Had the shooter just missed Paul because he had pulled the shot from his own inexperience or his own fear, or had he missed Paul because he hadn't wanted to kill him? If he had wanted to, he could have played a cat-and-mouse game with Paul and more than likely hunted him down.

He slept in an overstuffed chair in the living room with his feet on the coffee table. Twice he woke up in the night and wandered the house, staring out into the yard from each of the windows, trying to see if the man had returned. He wouldn't expect him to. Both now knew this game they played.

The rules to the game were fascinating. They included traveling across country to steal from Paul. They included returning to steal from Nora and then beat her up. Did they also include killing Chuck Owings? The committee was still out on that rule, but the decision on it would certainly change the game.

Previously published Worldwide Mystery titles by
TOM MITCHELTREE

A MERRY LITTLE CHRISTMAS
  in HOW STILL WE SEE THEE LIE (anthology)
KATIE'S WILL

katie's gold

Tom
Mitcheltree

WORLDWIDE®

TORONTO • NEW YORK • LONDON
AMSTERDAM • PARIS • SYDNEY • HAMBURG
STOCKHOLM • ATHENS • TOKYO • MILAN
MADRID • WARSAW • BUDAPEST • AUCKLAND

To:
Dorrie O'Brien, Feroze Mohammed,
Derek Lawrence, and perseverance
for helping me to be published.

KATIE'S GOLD

A Worldwide Mystery/July 2004

First published by Intrigue Press.

ISBN 0-373-26498-4

Printed in U.S.A.

katie's gold

ONE

RAIN FELL IN a penetrating mist that worked its way to his collar and seeped down his neck to his back. Even though it was late spring, the rain was still cold, so he hunched over a little more and hurried a little faster, hardly a romantic image dashing across campus. Hardly the image he had imagined for himself a few years ago as he groomed himself to be a university professor.

Clutching his leather briefcase to his chest with one hand, he groped over his shoulder with the other until he found the hood to his jacket and pulled it up and over his head. Rain caught in the folds of the hood rolled down his face and soaked the rest of his collar.

"Damn it," he said. Two students walking ahead of him turned back to look at him. He felt sheepish. He knew them both.

"You should be used to this kind of weather in New England in the spring, Professor Fischer," one of them called out.

He acknowledged the comment with a weak smile and a slight wave of his hand. He was in no mood to discuss New England weather.

Paul hadn't planned on being in Maine, teaching at a private college. He'd planned to teach at Harvard or Yale, but, instead, he'd spent the previous year writing the biography of an obscure doctor from southern

Oregon as an excuse to keep himself occupied while his wife, from whom he was separated, decided what she wanted to do with her life. In the end she'd decided to stay with her female lover and divorce Paul.

That was not what he'd expected. He'd believed that in the end she would come to her senses, and come back to the marriage. He'd been so confident she'd be back, he was totally caught off guard when she'd informed him she'd filed the divorce papers, and that she and her lover would be moving to Pennsylvania where jobs waited both of them.

Paul had been playing catch-up ever since. He was forced to scramble to find a job. He started looking late in the school year. The one in Maine was the only offer he got that would be close enough for him to see his boys on any kind of a regular basis.

The boys... She'd gone for the divorce aggressively. She'd hired a lesbian lawyer who took the shirt off Paul's back and got custody of the boys for Beth before he'd had a chance to recover from the idea that she was serious. The quick move out of state made it almost impossible for him to contest the terms of the divorce. The fact that she had stripped him financially made it economically impossible for him to do more than follow her lead.

The rain came down harder now. He felt like breaking into a run, but he wasn't about to lose what little dignity he felt he still had by splashing across campus for all his students to see. The rain began to fall harder. He thought, what the hell. He didn't care what the students thought because more than likely he wouldn't be back. He had applied to a number of colleges and universities that would pay more money than this one, and if any of them came back with an offer, he would be gone.

He loped across campus with his briefcase clutched to his chest. He wanted to be back in his apartment as quickly as possible, in dry clothes with his warm slippers on his feet. He'd had enough of Maine, he'd had enough of his former wife, and he'd had enough of this college. Professors grew old, fat, and content here. It was a place for men and women who lacked ambition. He had a future in education, but it wasn't one that could be made here.

He stopped running when he reached the gate outside his apartment. He lived in half of the bottom floor of a house that had been converted into a four-plex. Because the house was located close to campus, and because it had been remodeled, he didn't need to worry about sharing the space with students. The rent was too high. He shared it with three other teachers at the college, two men and a woman.

He closed the gate behind him and took his key out to open the front door. The door opened onto a hallway and stairway. The hallway passed through to the back of the house. He and his neighbor downstairs had doors opposite each other. At the top of the stairs, the two other neighbors had the same. Inside, he slipped his key into the lock and opened the door. As dim as the living room was in the fading afternoon light, he knew immediately a disaster had taken place. The room was filled with shadows that should not have been there, shadows cast from books dumped on the floor from the bookcase. Shadows cast by overturned lamps and furniture. Shadows cast by curtains torn and pulled away from the windows.

He stood in the doorway and listened. The room was silent, but he wasn't sure that someone wasn't still inside, waiting motionless, listening for his next move. He made the wisest move he could. He closed the door to his apartment and stepped across the hall to his neighbor's door and rang the bell. When the woman answered, he asked to use the phone to call the police.

TWO

HE WAITED IN the hallway until the two police officers had surveyed the damage in his apartment and then told him that it was okay for him to come in.

"We will need for you to tell us what is missing, Mr. Fischer," one of them said.

He started in the living room at the front of the house, trying to remember just exactly what it was he had that a thief might have taken. It wasn't as simple as it should have been. Both his television and video recorder were still in place. The CD player had been pulled off the bookshelf, but it was on the floor on top of a heap of books. Even his camera was on the floor, close to the shelf where he kept it.

The living room, dining room and kitchen were all open to each other. On the outside wall were French doors that led to a patio, screened from the street by a high fence and tall shrubs. This was the way the thieves came in. They had simply popped out a pane of glass in one of the doors and reached inside to unlock it.

The kitchen and dining area had been treated more gently. Drawers had been pulled open, cupboard doors left ajar, some of the dry food pulled out and dropped to the floor, but little else had been done in here. They weren't looking for the silver, he mused. Besides, Beth had it anyway.

A short hallway led to the two bedrooms in the back of the house. In between were a bathroom and a laundry room across from each other. Again, both of those rooms had been gone through, but not with the same devastating search that the living room had undergone.

His own bedroom had been tossed, literally. All of his clothes had been tossed from the dresser and the closet onto the bed and floor. The night stands had been gone through and even the mattress on the bed folded over to see what was underneath. He must have disappointed them. No gold coins hidden under the bed, no folded wad of money hidden with the socks, and no pictures of naked women under his mattress.

The second bedroom, the one he used for his office, got the worst of it. His computer had been shoved off the desktop onto the floor. The content of all the desk's drawers had been dumped on top of the desk. His two, four-drawer filing cabinets had been emptied, the contents flung around the room so that he waded ankle deep in papers. Books had been pulled from the shelves in the room and dumped on the floor.

He stared for a long time at all of it. The things of value in the room: the computer, the printer, and another CD player, were all there—on the floor. The only other thing of value he had was his laptop computer, and that was in his leather briefcase.

He turned back to the cop standing in the doorway behind him. "I don't know what's missing," he said. "Until I can sort through all this, I won't know. All the things you would think a thief would steal are still here, though."

The cop nodded. "It is possible you got home when the thieves were still here," he said. "They might not have had time to haul anything away."

Paul nodded, but he didn't believe that for a minute. His neighbor had been home for a half an hour before Paul arrived, and she hadn't heard a thing. Besides, as soon as Paul called the police, he took a tour around the outside of the house. He'd found no sign of anyone making a hurried getaway.

The two officers compiled a few notes and then left, basically telling Paul that even if something was missing, the chances of catching the thieves were thin. They could send back an investigator to dust for fingerprints, but even the dumbest crooks had watched enough movies to know to wear gloves.

With nothing of value apparently missing, Paul could not think of a reason for a further investigation. He did call his insurance agent, who came over and took some pictures, and then Paul began the laborious task of putting everything back in place. Only then would he know if something really was missing or not.

He worked well into the night. His neighbor across the hall, Jane Peters, an associate professor of Eastern Religions, brought him soup and sandwiches for dinner. If she hadn't knocked on his door with the offering, he wouldn't have thought about food. He was too busy, as he picked up books off the floor, wondering why someone would break in and not steal anything of value.

Jane stayed to help for awhile. She had a discussion group that she led two evenings a week, and this was one of the evenings. She was not only a steadying influence for him that night, but she had been for the whole year. A little older than Paul, and also divorced, she had proven to be both good company and a good friend. Early in their relationship, they had made the mistake of going to bed with each other, and it had been a disaster. She wasn't really looking for a man, and he wasn't really interested in a sexually complicated relationship. That night had left a little frost between them. It thawed quickly enough, and in the end, they settled on being good friends.

She was the one who suggested that the thief might have been looking for a copy of his final examination papers. He was teaching three literature courses this semester, and not all of his students were having an easy time of it.

"If that's what they were looking for," he said, "then I won't find anything missing. I never use the same test twice, and I haven't made up the tests for these classes yet."

"I wish I could be as well unorganized as you are," Jane said.

By midnight he had everything back in place. The computer monitor now had a roll to the screen he couldn't stop, but everything else seemed to have survived the search and still worked. Nothing appeared to be missing.

He slept fitfully that night, but he still managed to be up by seven-thirty and outside his office on campus an hour later. His office was in a two-story brick building set off from the other buildings on campus. In it were dozens of small offices for the associate professors. Only full professors got office space in the building where they taught. The underlings were left to dash through the rain from building to building where their various classes were located.

That was another reason Paul wanted to leave this school. Tenure meant power. The gap between the haves and the have-nots was a chasm. He wasn't given much of a chance to impress the elite on campus. Other than at a few highly structured faculty parties, the haves and the have-nots were kept well apart from each other, so much so that the department meetings were not meetings at all, but lectures given by the tenured staff members to the associates. The associates were expected to take notes.

He pushed open his office door and thought for a moment of *déjà vu*. Everything in the small room that had been so carefully organized was now in a heap on the floor. He picked up his phone from the floor and called Security. He then stepped outside of his office and waited for help to arrive.

THREE

CAMPUS SECURITY was about as helpful and optimistic as the local police department. An officer surveyed the damage, took a few photos and wrote some notes. He seemed more concerned about whether or not Paul had locked his door than he was about something being missing.

If something was missing, it would be the afternoon before Paul could find out. He had a ten o'clock class to teach, nineteenth century literature. This certainly was not his favorite class to teach, the emphasis on Classicism and Romanticism, but as an associate professor he wasn't given much in the way of choices of what he would teach.

Today was a review before the final examination next week. Paul couldn't help but move from face to face in his classroom, wondering if one or more of his students had been the ones to break into his apartment and his office. Instead of a hint of guilt on faces, he saw what he normally saw: a few students diligently taking notes, a few more listening with mild interest, and a few more fighting to stay awake. He often mused that if he graded on the attention paid in class, the end results for grades in the class would not be much different from the ones he would get on the final examination.

When he returned to his office and surveyed the mess,

he felt relief that he had already graded and returned the term papers for his classes, so they weren't mangled in the debris on the floor. Cleaning up the shambles in his office took longer than his apartment had taken. He was comfortable being less structured and organized at home, but in his office he demanded order of himself. Most of his books were here, as well as his research material for dozens of papers he had written. He always wanted to be able to put his hand on a book or a paper quickly because he was afraid any delay would shatter a line of thought. Even though he might well be packing all of this up within a month or two, he still put it all back in place, carefully sorted, ordered and alphabetized.

After he had finished, late in the afternoon, he was able to ease himself into the chair behind his desk and lean back to relax. The hours of labor and the thought that went with it produced little in the way of clues. His research material was simply too extensive to know if something was missing or not. He'd have to need it, look for it, and find it gone before he would know for sure that it was missing. Still, something seemed missing, although it wasn't the computer in the room, or the CD player, or any of the other kinds of gadgets that a thief might take if he was robbing for the sake of robbing.

One idea had flickered through his mind, although it made no sense at all. He wondered if this might have something to do with Beth. He couldn't imagine a reason for her to be behind a break-in to his office and apartment, but nothing else made much sense, either. He remembered as he was cleaning that he'd told his students he'd be spending the weekend making up their tests, after he had time to absorb what he had learned from their research papers. The obvious thought that someone had broken into these two places looking for the final examination paper looked unlikely at the moment.

He picked up the phone and called. When Denise answered, he didn't even flinch. He supposed that for most people there was a point in a divorce when it became obvious that a marriage had failed and nothing more could be done to revive it. That had finally happened to him, and when it did he no longer resented Denise, his wife's lover, nor cared what the two of them might do together behind locked doors. He was more concerned about the good mental health of his boys, but so far a series of counseling sessions involving all of them had seemed to blunt the worst of it for them.

Beth came on the line, sounding friendly as always. Once she'd been sure she was going to get her way, she had relaxed with him. "Hi," he said. "How's everything?"

"Fine," she said. "You should be ending the term soon. Will you be coming to see the boys?"

He delayed the question he really wanted to ask. "I thought I might have them up here for a couple of weeks after classes are out."

"What, so they can watch you work?"

"As a matter of fact, I'm not going to teach over the summer. I've lined up some interviews, but that's all."

"Interviews?"

"I'm still looking for the right teaching position," he said. "This isn't it."

"I don't think you'll ever settle down," she said.

He didn't pursue the subject, a sensitive one for both of them. They had lived a typically nomadic life of a student seeking the kinds of credentials that would lead to a teaching position in a top university. That meant a bachelor, masters and doctorate degree from three widely flung universities. It meant time out for research in far-off places, including several trips overseas for two to four months at a stretch. Although Beth picked up some credits along the way, she spent most of the time being a wife and then a mother. She was just now completing her education with Denise's strong support, as she had reminded Paul on more than one occasion.

"When do the boys get out of school?" he asked.

"Not for another two weeks," she said. "I may as well prepare you," she added. "They aren't going to want to come up there. They both want you to come here."

He fought back the anger. Because she had custody of the boys, she had leverage that was almost unfair, he felt. She could manipulate them on a daily basis, and he could only be a passing influence on their lives. "Why's that?" he asked, keeping the anger out of his voice.

"They've signed up for both summer soccer and baseball. I also have them swimming and taking tennis lessons. I thought you'd approve."

Beth was always clever at manipulating him. She was keeping the boys for the summer, against his wishes, because they were going to be doing things he'd want them to do. To fight it would not only disappoint the boys, but confuse them. How could he object to them playing soccer and baseball?

"Of course," he said. "We couldn't have them up here."

"I recognize that tone of voice, Paul. Maybe we should talk later."

This was something new she'd inserted into her arsenal. When he touched on something she didn't want to talk about, she'd politely hang up on him. If it were an issue that needed resolution, he would either hear from Denise or Beth's lawyer. She was determined to make sure that they never reached any level of intimacy again, and in her book, fighting was a form of intimacy.

"I do get the feeling that you're afraid to have them with me for any length of time, as if I might undo some mind control you've exerted over them."

Instead of getting angry, as he expected her to, she laughed. "You certainly don't know very much about your boys. In their ways, they are as willful as you are."

If she laughed at his best shot, she was sure of herself. That meant the boys stayed with her. He thought this was the perfect time to catch her off-guard. "Both my office and apartment were broken into during the last twenty-four hours. You wouldn't know anything about that, would you?"

Without a moment of pause, she started to laugh again, a deep, rich laughter, completely sincere. When she got herself down to giggles, she finally said, "I'm sorry to laugh, but as good as my lawyer is, what is there left?"

Indeed, he thought, what was left to take? He couldn't even be mad at her for laughing. They'd been a nomadic family with little time or money for accumulating possessions. She'd kept what little furniture they'd had. He paid child support and took care of school and insurance costs. She asked for some financial help while she finished school. He did not resent her that. He still made enough to get by. "I'm trying to eliminate possibilities," he said. "I just want to make sure you know of no reason why someone would want to rob me."

"I haven't got a clue," she said. "What did they take?"

It was his turn to laugh. "So far, I don't know," he said. "They didn't take any of the obvious things you'd expect thieves to take, and they didn't seem to be after stuff like test papers.''

"Maybe someone just wants to make your life as uncomfortable as he thinks you've made his. Do you have any disgruntled students?"

"All of my students are disgruntled. They would prefer that their grades be based on attendance, a nice smile, or a modest show of attentiveness. They resent the work they have to do for the grade. But, I don't ask anything more of them than any other professor would, and I don't ridicule them, or threaten them, or seduce them. I slip in the dagger with a smile on my face, and they never feel the pain until after the grade cards come out."

"Are you sure teaching is the right thing for you? You've become cynical at an early age."

"All teachers are cynical at the end of May. In the fall they are born-again optimists. It's part of the miracle of time off."

"I wish the rest of us were so lucky. Well, sorry. I haven't got a clue. I didn't send Denise to Maine with black grease paint on her face in the middle of the night to rob you of your riches. I was the most valuable thing you had, and you squandered that. 'Bye.''

As he put down the phone and shoved it back in place at the corner of his desk, he stopped, arms extended, and stared in amazement. Slowly he let his mouth shut and rose to look around the room. He even got on the floor and poked around under his desk. Convinced he was right, he got up and stood in the middle of his office trying to figure out what it might mean.

The one object missing from his desk was a gold-framed picture of Kate Baker. Why on earth, he wondered, would anyone want to steal that?

FOUR

HE DIDN'T NEED the picture of Kate Baker that had been on his desk to recall the beauty of the incredible blonde who'd thrown his life for a loop nearly two years before. He leaned back in his chair and remembered.

He had gone to Jacksonville, Oregon, to write a biography about Doc Hollingsworth. He had no idea at the time that he had been tricked, drawn into a plot conceived by Pam Livingston, Nora Ryan, and Chuck Owings. They were behind the grant to write the biography, but they had no interest in Hollingsworth. What they wanted was information about the Bakers: Emily, Elizabeth, and Kathryn.

The reason they wanted the information was simple enough. Although Kate had done her best to divest the Baker estate of its money before she died, she still managed to leave millions behind. Pam Livingston wanted to prove that she had a claim to the money, but being the lawyer who managed the estate put her in a difficult position. Anything she did to prove her claim to the estate would be questioned. That's why the three of them decided to lure a researcher to the valley and trick him into writing about the Bakers.

He smiled to himself. "Trick" wasn't the right word in his case. After seeing the picture of Kate Baker he knew he couldn't but write about the beautiful woman with the fascinating history. He did write about the Baker sisters, too, after finding out all that the others could not. Then, in the end, almost inexplicably even to himself, he had hidden the manuscript and all the research he'd discovered, leaving Pam's proof, metaphorically, in Kate Baker's care.

Pam Livingston was a little piqued when he left but determined as ever to prove her case, even after Paul left the valley. That didn't surprise him. She would be doomed to start each day looking in the mirror and wondering why she was the near duplicate of Kate Baker in appearance when Kate was only supposed to be her very distant aunt.

Nor should it have been, he thought, but without his research, Pam Livingston couldn't prove a thing.

He got up from the desk and began to make a systematic search of the office. A half hour later, he'd confirmed his suspicion that the picture was gone. All of the research material on Doc Hollingsworth, the only material he had brought back with him from Oregon, was also gone. Even one of the copies of the Doc's biography he'd written was missing from the bookshelf.

He was equally as sure that whatever papers he might have had about the doctor would be missing from his apartment. Perhaps Pam Livingston had hit a brick wall. Perhaps now she was desperate for the materials she suspected he had.

Paul looked out the window. Night had fallen and he'd missed it. A Friday night and he was still at work in his office. Somehow, only a few years before, he had expected his life to be much different from what it had become.

He gathered up the few things he wanted to take back to the apartment and locked the office securely behind him. The campus police assured him that his office would be well-watched over the weekend, another case of closing the gate after the horse was gone. The local police had assured him that a patrol car would pass his apartment on a regular schedule as well.

Outside, he paused and smelled the night air. The rain had scoured the smell of the town from the air, and now he only could smell spring. In it was the smell of grass growing, flowers blooming and leaves budding. Because of the aromas in the air, he felt a longing. Spring was the season for lovers, and he was no different from them. Now that he had broken the bond with Beth, he wanted someone to replace it. He couldn't think of love without thinking about Pam Livingston. They had shared a bed together.

He nodded his head a bit as he walked. It had been a great lie. She was trying to work him to get information about Kate Baker. He was embracing Kate Baker, or at least Kate Baker incarnate. Still, despite the lies on both sides, the moment had been... Had been... Well, it had simply been worth its billing. Pam was a gorgeous creature... For those moments she had been Kate Baker.

He followed the sidewalk through a small park, no more than a grove of trees with a winding path in the midst of them. He had gone about twenty feet when suddenly a dark figure came hurtling out of the shadows and crashed into him. He was so caught up in the memory of Pam Livingston that he was literally flying through the air before he had a clue of what was happening to him.

Paul hit the ground first, and then the body slammed down on top of him. The driving weight of the other man crushed the breath out of Paul. He curled up in a defensive posture and sucked hard to draw air into lungs that didn't seem to want to work. In those seconds the other man was up and running. By the time Paul rolled over enough to see, the man was gone. The only thing he had seen in the few seconds was a fleeting vision of a shadow.

When he could, after the air had finally returned to his lungs, he sat up. The woods around him were silent. The path, dimly lighted, was deserted. The only noises he could hear were distant and indistinct. He stood up and surveyed the damage. His overcoat had some mud and bits of debris on it. Nothing seemed to be damaged or even sore. In fact, it all could just as easily have been a dream, except for the one fact: His briefcase was gone.

He brushed himself off as best he could, and then he walked slowly back to the apartment, making sure he kept himself well in the light and on a path traveled by others.

He mourned the loss of the leather briefcase. It had been one of the last presents Beth had given him. Other than that, though, he hadn't lost a thing. The briefcase was nearly empty. He had left his portable computer and papers in his office, not needing them because all of his grading was done except for the finals, which wouldn't be taken until next week. Somebody got a nice briefcase but little else.

On a whim, he walked two blocks past his apartment to another house, this one a one-family dwelling with a single-car garage standing alone near the street. The house was owned by a retired professor, a woman who believed in public transportation and not in automobile ownership. As a result, she had no use for the garage. Paul rented it from her for his lovely old Volvo, a two-door sedan from the '60s that still carried the curves the car manufacturer had abandoned in later years.

A quick tug on the lock that secured the double doors of the garage confirmed what he had suspected. The lock swung open. He lifted it off and pulled one of the doors back. Since the lock was unsecured but still in the latch, he knew no one would be in the garage. He found the string hanging down near the door frame. It was threaded through several metal eyes to the naked bulb in the center of the ceiling. He gave the string a pull and the light came on.

After a quick look, he decided that it could have been worse. Whoever had broken into the car had used some kind of a lock-breaker to open the driver's door and the trunk. The paint hadn't even been scratched, and a fair mechanic could probably fix any damage done to both locks in short order. He didn't spend much time on the car. The radio, an original AM model, was still in place. He had nothing else in the car worth stealing.

Paul walked back to the garage doors and closed the one he'd opened. Still inside with the car, but no longer visible from the street, he worked his way up the passenger side to an area in front of the garage where there was room for a little storage and a workbench. He'd stacked the Volvo's four snow tires next to the bench when he'd pulled them off the month before and put on regular tires. He reached through the center of the tires to the third one down, then groped around the inside of that one until he found the small box. He pulled it out.

It was still securely wrapped in the cloth he had put around it for insulation. He doubted that the temperatures in the garage would hurt the disks inside, but he was a little concerned about moisture getting inside the box. Computer disks were pretty hardy items, but he wasn't going to take any chances.

He put the box back inside the tire. Perhaps he had

become overly cautious, but his experience in Jacksonville had been an eye-opener for him. He had not imagined before then the extremes that basically honest, intelligent, and successful people would go for money. He had been tricked once. He would not be tricked again.

He turned out the light to the garage and shut the door behind him, re-locking the lock that had been picked but not broken. Paul knew one thing for sure: Whoever was going through his things knew how to get in apartments, offices, and garages. He also knew how to do it without creating a lot of interest from the police. Paul could see himself calling in to tell the cops that his car and garage had been entered, that his empty briefcase had been stolen, and some research material had been taken that was basically duplicated in the dozen copies of his book that the thief had left behind. If anything, the cops would start wondering what it was he had that someone was so desperate to get. Paul couldn't answer that for sure, but he could imagine that the police, being police, would think drugs. Drugs were the least of Paul's problems.

Walking back to his apartment, he thought about the disks in the garage. They contained the research materials for the book about Doc Hollingsworth. He'd wanted an electronic record of what he'd done, one that could easily be accessed on a computer anywhere. He had scanned all the documents related to the doctor himself. He had the computer department at the university digitize and compress the photos he'd used. Because the files had been so large, he had invested in an external storage drive that had one-gigabyte disks for it.

Even though he had left the Baker sisters resting peacefully in their graves on the family estate outside of Jacksonville, that did not mean they had not traveled with him. A day did not go by when he was working on

the Hollingsworth book in which he did not think about
them. Because he was so distracted it had been easy for
Beth to go about the divorce in such a way that she got
all she wanted. He couldn't be bothered at the time. He
was too busy writing the Hollingsworth book and too
haunted by the Baker sisters to care what Beth was doing.

Although he had left behind all his research on them,
that didn't keep him from trying to get more information.
Away from Jacksonville, outside such a narrow scope of
focus, he had found out even more about the family.
Kate, herself a doctor, had kept in contact with her loyal
nurse who served by her side during World War I, even
after she returned to the Baker Ranch and disappeared
from the public's light. Paul had located the nurse's family and, much to his delight, discovered that Becky Mal-
doone, the nurse, had kept Kate's letters. Unburdening
herself to no one but her diary at home, Kate had re-
vealed even more in her letters to Becky. He'd even
learned a lot about Oliver Baker, the son she had given
up after birth. All that was on the disks, as well as the
information about the doctor. When he got back to his
apartment, he circled around the yard, peeking over the
fence to see what he could see. The patio doors were
shut, the glass in them intact.

He opened the door to his apartment and reached in
to turn on the light. He stood in the open doorway for
some time, straining to hear even the least bit out of
order. He left the door open and went through the apartment, flicking on all the lights and checking the windows
and patio doors. Convinced there were no intruders lurk-
ing about, he locked the front door and closed all the
curtains and blinds in the house.

In the living room he lighted the gas fireplace, the

fake logs looking more real than the real thing with none of the inconvenience. He then put on a CD by Kenny G. He stood for a moment and appreciated the mournful wail of the horn the artist played. After pouring himself a glass of wine, he sat in his overstuffed chair near the fire and put his feet up on the hassock that matched it. With only the light from the fire and with the music dancing in the background, he was now free to think this thing through.

The person who broke into his property was apparently after one thing. He took only the information about Doc Hollingsworth. That, of course, was not what the thief was after. Everything of interest about the doctor was in the book. The only material of interest about him that was not in the book was his relationship with the Bakers. That, Paul was sure, was the information the thief was after. The only person he could imagine desperate enough to get that information in an underhanded way was Pam Livingston, or, representing her, Nora Ryan and Chuck Owings.

He doubted that Nora Ryan would work on her own. In her sixties, she was the curator of the Jacksonville Museum, and she was Chin's granddaughter, a Baker servant. She was also Silas Baker's granddaughter, which Paul learned and documented, but which *she* still couldn't prove. He doubted that she had the resources to reach across country to try to get these papers.

Chuck Owings, on the other hand, did have the resources. A Medford city attorney, he'd been engaged to Pam before Paul came along. Paul guessed that the two were back together again. If Chuck were behind the break-ins, it had to be for Pam's benefit. Unless he was married to her, he couldn't touch the money himself.

He decided he'd give Pam a call in the morning just

to see if she might tip her hand about what she was up to. He refilled his glass of wine and put on a James Taylor CD, one a little less nerve-shredding than Kenny G's music.

He had reduced his thoughts to a fascination with the flicker of the flames when the phone beside him rang. He turned slowly to stare at it for a second, finally bringing it into focus. He glanced at his watch. It was after midnight. Phone calls after midnight were usually bad news or pranks. He had known both.

Paul let the answering machine get the call. When the voice came on after the beep, he was stunned. Just the sound of it flooded him with feelings he had forgotten he had. He leaned over and picked up the receiver.

"I was just thinking about you," he said.

She paused for several seconds before she responded. "I hope they were good thoughts," she said.

"If I try hard enough, I can drag up some of those."

"Don't strain yourself," she said.

"I've gotten past the strain. What is it you want, Pam?"

"Nora Ryan is in the hospital. She was assaulted in the museum records room. Someone stole all the information on the Bakers and Hollingsworth. What I want to know is: what are you up to, Paul?"

He couldn't help himself. As inappropriate as it was, he began to laugh.

FIVE

TWO MONTHS LATER, he leaned back in the airplane seat and wondered for the hundredth time if he was doing the right thing. One of the last things he'd ever expected to do was to return to the Rogue Valley and Jacksonville where he had first locked horns with Pam Livingston. He had won the first round, but the scars she left on him were deep and slow to heal. He wasn't sure that he had even scratched her lovely surface.

He had not planned on a trip to Oregon. He'd shared his experience about his break-ins with Pam to convince her that he had had nothing to do with Nora Ryan's problems. That might have ended the issue right there, but, although he hadn't talked to her in nearly two years, he felt a surge of excitement as they talked. Instead of having a cold, stilted conversation, one that he had imagined a dozen times before, they had a warm, animated discussion. At the heart of it were Nora Ryan's circumstances, but Kate Baker's image flickered at the edges.

Seeing Pam Livingston again no longer seemed as intimidating as it once had. And the few days that Paul had spent recently near Beth and the kids had made a visit to Oregon seem even more tempting. Beth treated him like a taxi service for the boys: ''Have them at the ball field at four. Have them on the soccer field at seven. Swim class starts at nine in the morning. They stay for

tennis afterward.'' On top of that was the constant re-
frain from the boys: ''Nobody else's dad stays for practice.''

Drive the boys around, but don't talk to them. Take
us where we need to go, but don't stay and watch what
we do. He'd given up the apartment in Maine. He'd
packed up his car and driven down to spend the summer
near the kids. Except the kids didn't want him too near,
Beth didn't want him there at all, and Paul wasn't much
into being a full-time chauffeur.

He'd already had two successful interviews, both in
New York State, and he was sure he'd get an offer for
a teaching position from one of them. Then he'd checked
with a placement service and found several college
teaching positions open in California. On a whim, he'd
sent off his résumé and lined up interviews. He'd then
called Pam Livingston and said he'd be coming to California for a couple of weeks. He left it open-ended, but
she'd quickly closed it for him. Something strange was
going on; she wanted him to come to Medford.

Paul had no trouble making a decision between being
a chauffeur, a second-class parent to his boys and a res-
ident in a motel for the summer, or a valued candidate
for a teaching position and someone needed to help solve
a mystery. He was off to California and Oregon.

Beth went through the ceiling. After seeing so little
of the boys in the last year, how could he abandon them
for the summer? He was being an irresponsible parent.
On top of that, he had no business going back to Oregon
where he had so deftly sabotaged his teaching future
with the worthless biography he had written. He needed
to get a decent teaching position and establish a solid
home base for his boys to visit. He didn't need to fly

back into the arms of the lawyer who, it appeared, had only manipulated him for her own ends.

In a calmer discussion, he might have agreed with Beth. He did need some stability in his life. He did need to provide a home for the boys when they came to see him. And, yes, as little as she knew about it, Beth was right about Pam Livingston. The lawyer had her own agenda.

But, given the choice of spending time with a woman he would never sleep with again and spending time with a woman he *might* never sleep with again, he chose Pam. Besides, he was curious. He would like to know who would reach all the way across the country to break into his apartment, office, and car to find out more about the Bakers. If it wasn't Pam, Nora, or Chuck, then who was this new player in the game? Whoever he was, he was proving every damned bit as dangerous as Pam Livingston and Chuck Owings had been.

He closed his eyes and let his mind wander over his memories of Jacksonville and the valley. The weather had been warm most of the time he was there. By East Coast standards, it had been hot, but the air was dry, so the heat didn't sap his strength. He had felt pleasantly baked, so that his body was always loose and limber. It had felt good.

He remembered the smells, too, a product of the heat. The air smelled of ripening fruit, and wheat, and grasses. What did not get watered or baked to a golden brown added to the aroma. Even the earth contributed. The soil had the moisture cooked out of it by the heat, and it took on a smell of its own that was as old as the Far West itself. The first time he had walked through the streets of the former, old gold-mining camp of Jacksonville, he had no trouble imagining himself walking the same streets a century before, about the time the Baker girls were going through their childhood.

He thought back to one of those warm days when he had sat on the low, stone-capped wall around the Jacksonville Museum, drinking a cup of coffee and soaking up the sun. At that moment he had felt a contentment he had never felt before. But, of course, that was before Pam Livingston and his involvement in the life of Kate Baker. He wasn't sure if he could recapture that feeling again.

He had his interviews first. He was determined to make them the focus of his trip and not the meeting with Pam Livingston. Deep inside, he was beginning to get the uneasy feeling that things had not been resolved between them, even though it seemed clear that they had at the time.

He knew what Pam wanted—proof that Oliver Baker had been Kate's son, which meant Pam was Kate's granddaughter, and heir to the Baker fortune. He was pretty sure he would not betray, even now, Kate Baker's will and give her the proof that she was Kate's granddaughter by letting Pam have the diaries Kate and her sisters had written so many years before. As beautiful and accomplished as Pam Livingston was, she was not Kate Baker.

Without the benefit of all the psychological advice offered by most talk shows on television today, Kate Baker had decided that a twisted strand ran through her family that would always emerge to destroy whatever chance of happiness any member might have. The strand was tied to land and wealth. She was determined to end it, to save her son from the misfortunes that came with it.

Kate had given Oliver to Silas's brother, Tim, to raise as one of his own shortly after Oliver's birth. Tim's wife, a chubby woman taken to flowing dresses, simply announced that the child was hers. Having made little issue with the pregnancies and births of her other children, all girls, the few people who saw her outside of church on Sundays, had little reason to doubt her word. The Bakers were an honest, hard-working couple, who made little money from farming but were generous with what they had. If Tim's wife said she had been pregnant under those flowing gowns, then she had been pregnant.

From what she knew of him before she died, Kate must have been proud of Oliver Baker, "Colonel O" as the men who served with him affectionately called him. Kate, Emily, and Elizabeth had done their part to keep Oliver's birth a secret. They rarely left the ranch and they paid the house help a tidy sum of money to keep quiet. Since this was at the end of the Victorian era, folks were pretty good at keeping hushed-up the things they didn't want people to know. And the staff at the Baker house was a very loyal one. Probably more loyal to Kate than the other two women.

Nora Ryan was Chin's grandchild, the housekeeper Silas Baker had impregnated, making Nora's mother illegitimate. Since Nora couldn't make a legal case for a piece of the Baker estate, she'd tied her star to Pam's, trying to help Pam prove that she was Kate Baker's granddaughter—for a price. That was it. Silas had no other lovers. Kate had no other children. Neither Elizabeth nor Emily had children. Oliver's only child was Pam. No one remained alive who could make a claim on the Baker estate, even if they did have the information that Paul had. No one, except for Pam Livingston and Nora Ryan.

Pam had never known her father; he'd been killed in Vietnam a few months before she was born. Her mother remarried, to a David Livingston, and he had adopted the fatherless girl. Paul did not know a lot about David Livingston, but he knew he was in real estate, and he had done well enough to provide handsomely for his family and send their only child, Pam, through law school.

Yes, as he thought about it, he was even more sure that no one else had a legitimate claim to Katie Baker's estate beyond Pam Livingston.

He smiled. She had made it clear to him when he left Oregon the last time that she would not give up trying to prove she had a claim to the estate. She seemed confident at the time. There was still a good chance she was manipulating him, trying one more time to get from him the information she needed.

He leaned back in his seat. For the first time since all of this began, he wondered what would happen if he let her have the diaries.

SIX

WHEN HE STEPPED FROM the plane into the airport terminal, he knew to what extent Pam Livingston had gone to deceive him. When he first saw her, his eyes lingered on her for a moment and then shifted beyond, looking for the Pam Livingston who was a near copy of Kate Baker. And then his eyes snapped back.

She had permed her hair in a way that gave it lots of body, making it resemble a blond, woolen mop. It had a certain disorder to it that, on her, had a wonderful attractiveness. She was now beautiful in a Meg Ryan sort of way instead of a Kate Baker way. The resemblance between Kate and Pam was still there, but harder to see. The difference in hairdos hid it, but the shorter, fuller style made Pam look more modern and young. She was, after all, a woman in her early thirties, who now perhaps was a little more aware of time slipping by than when he had first met her.

Paul was afraid this moment would be awkward for both of them. Pam took care of that. She stepped forward and took his hand and then pulled him slightly forward so she could kiss him lightly on the lips. They smiled at each other, a bit like old combatants who had never gotten the edge on the other but had from that experience gained a great deal of respect.

''How's Nora doing?'' he asked.

She let go of his hand and put an arm through his as they walked to the baggage area. "She's still not very clear about what happened. She suffered a severe concussion and was in a coma for several days after the attack. At first we didn't know what it was about. Only after her assistant had completed an inventory of the records room did we find out what was missing. That took several weeks."

"Is she still in the hospital?"

"No, she's back in her home, but she still hasn't gone back to work. I'm not sure she will."

He glanced at her, but he didn't see in her face the surprise he felt. Nora Ryan was an energetic woman, much younger than her years. He couldn't think of her not back in the museum. "I can't imagine Nora not going back to work," he said.

"She's changed," Pam said. "The assault was vicious; she's aged quite a bit."

They stood in the baggage area and waited for his luggage to arrive on a conveyer belt. "Have you any idea who did it?"

She glanced up at him and smiled. "My best guess was you."

"There was a time," he said, "when I could have killed her, but that time has passed."

"And killed me, too," she added.

He took time to admire her close up. She was dressed in a cream-colored business suit with a blouse of patterned pastels to match. With her blond hair and blue eyes, she was as pretty as any travel poster for a Caribbean island. "No," he said, shaking his head slowly, "I didn't want to kill you. I had too many feelings for you, some deserved and some not, but murder wasn't one of them."

She locked on to his eyes with hers, and said, with that edge of toughness he had been surprised to find in her when they first met, "If you expect an apology from me, don't. Personally, at the time I thought you were a fool who gave up too much and got too little in return. Kate Baker is dead, but you're not."

At the time she had offered him the rights to a book about the Bakers that would certainly have sold, and she offered him a piece of the money she would have gotten if he would prove her to be the heir to the Baker estate. He could have left the valley a rich man with a book behind him that would have him teaching at Harvard or Yale. He could even have had her, she had implied at the time.

And what had he gotten out of it? A teaching position no better than the last one he'd had. A divorce. Five hundred copies of a biography that no one wanted to read, most of the books sitting in boxes and gathering dust. He was free of the Kate Baker spell, but he was also free of the Pam Livingston spell. If he had been satisfied with the returns, he doubted that he'd be back here now.

He pulled his two suitcases from the conveyor belt. As they began walking toward an exit, he asked, "How's Chuck Owings?" His favorite memory of the district attorney was not of the night the man had held a gun to his head, but of the first time he had seen him in the lobby of Pam Livingston's office. He had been alive and full of energy, friendly and humorous. Paul liked to think that that was the way he really was when he wasn't conspiring with Pam and Nora.

"I don't know," she snapped. "How's your wife?"

"Ex, and not very happy that I'm back here."

She smiled without looking at him this time. "I know.

I talked to her while I was trying to track you down. She gave me a lecture about grabbing hold of a man before another woman was done with him.''

"Yes," he said, "we men are nothing but footballs waiting for a woman to run with us.''

She laughed. "Does she still have her woman friend?''

"I heard the boys refer to her once as 'Father Denise.' Yes, they seem to be doing okay together.''

"And the boys?''

"They're still mad at both of us, but this summer they're taking it out on me instead of her.''

She nodded. "That must be a hard one for them.''

"As best I can tell," he said, "it hasn't been much fun for any of us.''

She pulled her car keys from her purse as she guided him through the parking lot. "Chuck is still a city attorney, only in Washington State now instead of Medford. He lost a little interest in me when the promise of large amounts of money disappeared. Not a significant degree of interest, but enough for me to notice. He seemed pretty surprised when I sent him packing.''

They approached a maroon Mercedes, a more expensive model than the one she'd had last time he'd seen her. "Another nice car," he said. "A beautiful lawyer with a successful law practice and a lovely car. I would think Chuck Owings could be classified as certifiably crazy.''

She opened the trunk for his suitcases. As he put them in, she asked, "Then what does that make you? Add the adjective 'rich' to the above description. You could have had it all.''

He slammed the trunk lid. "Life is miserable and then you die," he said. "Who'd want it any other way?''

She rolled her eyes and then got into the driver's side of the car. He slipped in beside her. "Fischer, you just don't know how frustrated you made me. Don't be glib about it."

As she pulled from the parking lot, he asked, "Where are we going?"

"To my place," she said.

"I will need to find a place to stay."

"You'll be staying with me."

After a short pause, one long enough for a variety of possibilities to run through his mind, he said, "I'm not sure I'm ready for that."

She laughed. "In your dreams," she said. "I bought the house on Shady Lane. I told you I liked it. You'll be staying in the guesthouse."

"Oh," he said, suddenly feeling a little disappointed.

"You got in my bed once," she said, "but you will have to work a hell of a lot harder to get in there again."

He nodded. Fair enough, he thought. They were back to zero. No hard feelings; no good or bad points carried over from the last time. In fact, now the playing field was more even. She didn't have Chuck Owings sitting on the bench and he didn't have Beth. But the prize was still the same: Whoever won this match still took possession of the soul of Kate Baker.

"Who's doing the cooking?" he asked.

"Cooking's for the un-liberated. You've got a kitchenette in the guesthouse."

"That's what I liked about you," he said.

"What?"

"You always knew who you were, even if you couldn't prove it."

She pulled away from the airport and headed in the direction of Jacksonville in the northwest corner of the valley. "The money rightfully belongs to me," she said. "You know it. I know it. If you think I'm going to turn my back on millions because you have an over-developed sense of righteousness, you can forget it. I know I'm Kate Baker's granddaughter, even if I can't prove it yet—if for no other reason than I've got her kind of determination."

He didn't respond to the little outburst, nor did he think she expected him to respond. Yes, she was Kate Baker's granddaughter. One look at her confirmed that. The problem was, she was also a bit like Emily Baker, the one who wanted to control the Baker fortunes. And she had in her a bit of Elizabeth, the one who appeared to be innocent, but the one who was the most capable of being deceitful because of it. If she *were* pure Kate Baker, Paul would have helped her get the money.

She turned down Shady Lane and then turned again down the drive to the house nestled back among the orchards that bordered it on two sides and the long line of arborvitae that lined the driveway. The house had changed significantly since the last time he'd seen it. The driveway still circled around it to meet itself on the way out, but that was the only thing unchanged. The house now wore new colors, a pale blue with cream trim and dark shutters. Off the French doors was a new, expansive deck, complete with hot tub.

As they drove around behind the house and parked, he could see that the guesthouse had gotten the same treatment. Both had taken on a New England cottage look, and each cottage was now surrounded by extensive flower beds. The lawn was manicured. Everything about the grounds was picture-perfect.

As he got out of the car, he said, "Nice."

She joined him and looked around, nodding. "Yes, it

is. I pay a small fortune to a maintenance company to come in four times a month to keep it this way."

"And I thought you had grown a green thumb."

"I wish. Work allows me little time. At best I can take a stack of it out on the deck with me and at least smell the roses while I wade through it."

He walked back to the trunk of the car to get his bags. "I'm off for the summer. Eat your heart out."

"Statements like that make me want to eat your heart out. The guest cottage is unlocked. The key is on a hook next to the door. I put some TV dinners in the freezer and stocked the cupboards with the usual, so you won't starve. You have your own stereo, TV, and VCR. The only thing I can't provide you with is a car."

"After I get settled, if I can impose on you for a trip to a rental agency, your duties will be done."

She opened the door to the cottage for him so he could carry in his suitcases. "I can give you about an hour, and then I'll have to go back to work. I won't be home until about eight tonight, but I would like to talk about this Nora thing with you then."

He set the suitcases down in the living room. He admired the room. She had done an admirable job of decorating. She'd had a gas fireplace installed, surrounded by an antique mantle. The furniture was overstuffed. The walls were lined with shelves, paintings, and decorations. The room was almost cluttered, but tastefully so, and comfortably so, as well. The cottage had a bedroom, bathroom, and kitchen area with a dining table. He couldn't have asked for more, and the price was the best part of it.

"You've done a spectacular job of decorating," he said. "I can't wait to see the house."

"Antiques and clutter. You can hide a lot of faults with beautiful furniture and decorations."

"You sound just like a Baker," he said.

She leaned a shoulder on the doorframe and asked, "In what way?"

"They hid a lot of flaws behind their beauty, too."

SEVEN

THEY TALKED LITTLE as they drove into Medford to look for a car for him. Pam dictated notes into a handheld recorder.

He watched the scenery slip by. He couldn't help but look back to the north when they reached a stretch with an extended view, to see the glorious Victorian mansion on the distant hillside that had been the home of the Bakers. Kate had left in her will a large sum of money to maintain the house and the surrounding grounds, although the place was not to be opened to the public. Pam, as executor of the estate, had access to the house, and she had used that privilege to take Paul to it.

Like everything else from that time, the trip was planned to help Paul dig deeper into the Baker history. The one item in the house that Pam had not touched was Silas Baker's old safe. She had not found a way into it, and she hadn't had the courage to have it broken into. Such an overt act, she felt, might work against her if she tried to claim the Baker fortune.

Paul had gotten into the safe. He had learned long ago as a researcher that almost any information was out there if you tried hard enough to find it. The Baker sisters' three diaries were in the safe, put there in the end by Kate Baker. Careful to hide as much of the sisters' pasts as she could, and successful in destroying any record that Oliver Baker was actually her child, she was apparently incapable of destroying that last bit of information that represented all their lives. She preserved the diaries, but out of reach of the curious.

Pam did not know about the diaries, but she was sure that some record of her father's birth to Katie Baker existed. It did, in all three diaries. The three sisters each had her own view of that birth. For Kate the birth of the child was a reminder of the one great love she had in her life. For Emily, it was at first with hope that Oliver would be the boy child that her father had always wanted, the one to preserve the Baker empire, and then it was one of despair as she saw the child given up to their uncle to raise as his own. Elizabeth met the birth of the child with pure jealousy. *Kate* had the child *she* was never to have. She never got past resenting Oliver's birth enough to care what became of the child after he was born.

Paul decided that once they finished with the business of Nora Ryan, he would tell Pam bits and pieces of her relatives, especially her father. When she had enough of the story, he would then decide from her reactions whether or not he would give her the diaries, the ones he still had—sort of. He had wrapped them to be watertight and had carefully placed them in a plastic box, and then he had buried them next to Kate Baker's headstone in the graveyard located in the front yard of the house on the hill.

In town, he suddenly asked her to stop the car. "What?" she asked, as she pulled over to the sidewalk. "We're still blocks from Avis."

He pointed at a sign that said Rent-A-Wreck. "Don't ask," he said.

"Hey," she said, "if you need some financial help renting a car—"

He held up a hand to stop her. "I just went a year spending almost no money on myself. I'm not hurting. Ever since I first heard about these places, I wanted to rent a car from them."

Her head tilted a bit to one side, appraising him. "I really don't know you," she said. "I was sure I did at one time, but you quickly proved me wrong. Even now you can surprise me."

"I always wanted to be a mystery to someone," he said. "Beth was sure she knew everything she wanted to know about me."

"I'm not Beth," Pam said. "Don't make comparisons. And I'm not Kate Baker. I am Pam Livingston, and I'm not totally uncomfortable with it."

"You shouldn't be," he said. "I'm sorry you can't be satisfied with it."

"Fair enough."

He got out of the car and then bent down to say goodbye. "I'll see you later tonight."

"Okay. By the way, I always wanted to rent from one of these lots, too. I saw a VW convertible on one once, and thought that would be renting in style."

Paul didn't get a VW. Instead, he settled for a nice 1988 Alfa Romeo Spider. He didn't care for the rubber nose added to it or the rubber spoiler which tarnished the lines of a sports car he considered to be a beauty in its classic form, but the car was black, too, so the add-ons weren't so noticeable.

As soon as the paperwork was completed, he pulled off the lot and headed back the way they had come earlier. Only this time he wasn't going back to Pam's, he was going to Jacksonville. He wanted to see Nora Ryan on his own.

Paul had expected Nora's house to be one of the ones with a plaque on the outside proudly displaying the date of its construction like so many of the historical houses in Jacksonville. Instead he found that her address led him out of town on the old Stagecoach Road, and then right, up into a valley filled with new houses. Her house sat up on a ledge that gave it a view of the Rogue River Valley and the Table Rocks beyond.

He parked his car on the street and climbed a long set of steps that rose from the street to the house above. A winding walkway led to the front door. He rang the doorbell and stood on the porch for some time, waiting for an answer. He rang it again and then turned to stare out across the valley.

As he stood there, a man from the house across the street came out of his garage, walked the length of the driveway, crossed the street, and climbed up the steps to meet Paul. He didn't say a word, but simply stopped a few feet away.

The front door opened behind Paul. He turned around to see Nora Ryan. Or at least to see someone who looked like a much older version of Nora. This woman drooped at the shoulders, and the lines on her face were much deeper. Her hair was completely white, instead of still mostly dark and streaked with gray. "Nora?" Paul asked.

"I thought it was you," the woman said, and then she nodded to the man behind Paul. Paul glanced back to see the man retreat the way he had come, still without saying a word.

"Anyone I should know?" he asked.

"He's a Jacksonville cop. He's keeping a good eye on me. He comes when I call."

He now understood what Pam meant when she said that Nora might not return to work. She had aged at least twenty years since the last time he'd seen her. "How are you doing, Nora? I heard you've had a bad time of it."

"There was a time when I thought maybe you knew I was going to have a bad time of it before I did," she said, her voice flat, her expression missing the owlish, impish quality it once had. Now she wouldn't look directly at him. "Don't expect me to invite you in. I'm still not convinced you weren't somehow involved, trying to get even or something."

"I assure you that I was three thousand miles away when you were attacked. I can prove that."

"But can you prove you didn't hire someone to do it?"

"After my divorce, Nora, I couldn't afford to hire someone to walk across the street for me. Besides, why would I do that? I had all the information I needed. I've even found out a little more since I last saw you."

He threw in that last bit as a teaser. Nora before had been as desperate to find out about the Bakers as Pam. She wanted every piece of information he had. Instead of rising to the bait, she dismissed it.

"Good riddance to the Bakers. If this is what I get out of it, I don't want to know anything more about them."

Because she was getting agitated, and because the cop across the street still stood in the open doorway to the garage keeping an eye on them, Paul decided to shift gears for a minute to try to calm her down. "I expected you to live in one of those historical houses in Jacksonville," he said.

She stared off across the valley. Finally she said, "I used to. Then when Jacksonville became 'quaint' and 'in,' I sold it for a lot of money and bought this place. I was glad to let someone else worry about the fact the house needed a foundation, and that the walls had no insulation, and the wiring dated back to the nineteen-thirties, and the water and sewage lines would all need to be replaced."

"I never thought about that."

"You've never spent a winter here with cold, wet air seeping through the cracks in the walls."

"No, I haven't had that chance yet. On the other hand, I do have an interview at the university in Ashland. I'm due for a change in my life."

"Divorce will do that," she said.

"It does have a way of derailing your plans. Now, do you want to tell me about the break-in? I don't know if Pam told you or not, but my house, office, and car were broken into back in Maine. And I was knocked down and my briefcase stolen while I was walking home. Whoever did it was looking for information about the Bakers."

"That's what Pam said. I didn't believe it at the time, so I had my neighbor check. He said police reports were filed on your house and office."

He nodded, surprised that she would go to so much trouble. "I didn't bother to report the other two. Nothing was taken from my car and my briefcase was empty."

"And you don't have a clue who'd have done it?"

"Not a clue."

She nodded. "That's about what I can tell you. I went back to work late one night. Someone died and left us an attic full of junk. I still needed to get it sorted. Storage is such a problem at the museum. I no more than got in my office when I was slammed into the wall. I must have been knocked out because when my head first cleared I didn't know where I was.'' She still didn't look at him, but continued to stare out across the valley as if she was seeing on the distant hills what had happened to her. ''When I finally had it together again, I could see the light was on in the records room. Like one of those stupid women in those horror films, instead of running out the door as fast as I could, I walked into the room. I guess I thought he'd be gone.''

''Was there just one?''

''That was all that I saw. He was at the computer. Black clothes. Black stocking cap. Latex gloves on his hands. I must have made a noise. He was cat-quick. I know he hit me two or three times. The doctor says more. I just know he made sure I wouldn't get up again.''

''Did you see his face?''

''Just a blur of it,'' she said. ''I saw his eyes, though. They were dark and angry. The one thing that was missing from them was fear.''

What was there for him to fear? She was, after all, an old woman. ''Would you recognize him again if you saw him?''

She shook her head slowly. ''I'll never see him again. I'll never want to. The doctor said it was a miracle that I survived the beating. He hit me and kicked me. He didn't pull any punches; he could just as easily have killed me.''

It was not difficult seeing that she believed that. Paul didn't know if that was the victim speaking or the truth. ''Are you going back to work?''

For the first time she looked directly into his eyes. "The man is after something. If he didn't get it from me, and he didn't get it from you, he'll keep trying until he does get it. If he thinks he missed something, he'll be back. He's never catching me off-guard again. But I suggest you watch your back."

A chill ran up his spine. He thought of how it might have been if the body hurtling at him in the park had been armed with a knife. If this was the same man, the one who didn't mind beating an old woman severely enough to kill her, he wouldn't think twice about killing someone like Paul.

"I'll do that," he said.

She turned back to her door and opened it, turning around again before she went inside. "Pam has you staying at her house for a reason. She thinks your presence will discourage the man from coming after her. You don't look like you could protect yourself, let alone her." She disappeared inside and shut the door behind her.

If that was Pam's plan, he thought, she was going to be disappointed. The man had come after him once already, and nothing from that encounter would discourage him from coming back again.

The neighbor kept on eye on him until he drove the Alfa out of view. As he drove back to the house on Shady Lane, he thought about what Nora had said. Who would know which people had information about the Bakers, and how would he know it? The only person he could think of was Chuck Owings.

But what was in it for him? If he and Pam had split up, then there shouldn't be anything in it for him. Unless, of course, they hadn't split up. These three had roped him into their scheming once before. Perhaps all of this was another clever attempt to get the information from him they couldn't get before.

He decided he might take a trip to Washington to talk to Owings, just to see what the former DA might have to say.

EIGHT

THE LAST THING that Chuck Owings was thinking about was Pam Livingston and Katie Baker. He had just gotten a conviction in a tough child molestation case, the kind of case that might make a district attorney a candidate for a state representative. Chuck didn't plan to stay in Tacoma forever as a DA. Like Medford, this was a stepping stone to better things.

He moved quickly down the steps to the sidewalk, agile for a big man in his forties. He took a lot of pride in staying fit. He worked out at a health club four times a week, and he took three-mile walks on the off days. He wasn't ashamed to admit that he did a little touch-up on his hair, and he spent a little extra money on suits cut to make him look great. After all, he was now long-divorced and suddenly free since he and Pam Livingston parted company. He had been a bit shaken when they split up, but he found soon enough that life for an eligible bachelor with a handsome salary, even one over forty, was pretty darned good. He'd had enough conquests recently to make life very interesting indeed.

He found his BMW convertible waiting for him in the parking lot, looking every bit as good as it had the first time he'd seen it in a showroom. This was the perfect car. A Ferrari would have been too much. A Miata convertible would have been too little. This had the nice combination of good looks, high price, and conservatism. Any woman who didn't appreciate it, he figured, wasn't worth his time.

He would like to go back to the office to gloat over his victory in court, but he had a hot date tonight with a woman from his club. He didn't know a lot about her, other than she looked terrific in a pair of tights, she was single, and she drove a Lexus. He'd been trying to get her to go out with him for a month, and now the date was a bonus to go with his court win.

He didn't have far to drive. His condo was close to the city park, near enough to an upscale part of town to be just the right neighborhood for his position. He waited for the guard to the parking garage to wave him through, then he entered and found his parking spot. Within a few minutes the elevator deposited him on the top floor, which he shared with a half a dozen successful professionals in the city. He had a corner apartment that overlooked the park.

He let himself in through the double doors and set his briefcase down on a chair in the large entrance hall. He took the doorway to the right and walked into the living room, turning on lights as he went. The living room offered a two-sided view of the park. Behind it was the dining room, also with a view, and then the kitchen area. The other half of the apartment had three bedrooms and two baths. He used one of the bedrooms as a den.

In the master bedroom he pulled off his tie and shirt and headed to the bathroom to freshen up before his date. He stood in front of the mirror and patted his flat belly, feeling good about it. Only someone his own age could appreciate how much harder he had to work than his younger acquaintances to stay this fit. It required a great deal of exercise and a fanatic's approach to diet.

Only on nights like this, when he was going out to dinner, did he violate his diet. He didn't want the rest of the world to know how hard he worked.

He again admired his physique in the mirror, smiling at what he saw, and then the smile froze on his face as a figure in black slipped up behind him in the mirror. He started to turn around but was stopped by the barrel of a gun pressed deep into the soft spot just below his left earlobe.

A voice, deep, nondescript, and accent-free, told him to put his hands on the bathroom counter, palms down, flat. He did as he was told, watching the man behind him. He guessed him to be about six-two, his own height, and maybe twenty pounds heavier, all of it appearing to be muscle. The man's head was covered with a black ski mask so the only features Chuck could identify were cold, gray eyes, and thin, pale lips.

"My wallet is on the dresser," Chuck said.

"Goody," the voice said, heavy on sarcasm. "I'm sure it's long on credit cards and short on cash." He stepped back from Owings. "Now, I'm going to back out of the bathroom and I want you to back out as well. This is a nine-millimeter, fourteen-shot automatic with a silencer. A slight twitch from you and you'll get a half a clip before you hit the floor."

Chuck backed out of the bathroom, awkwardly. He felt a flutter of fear when he lost the image of the man in the mirror. Now he had no idea of what was going on behind him. "I want you on your stomach on the bed with your hands behind you," the voice said.

Chuck did as he was told. Something slipped over his hands and then his wrists were yanked tightly together. Before he could recover from the sharp pain of it, the same thing happened at his ankles. He was able to glance down and see that the man had used notched, plastic ties on him, the same heavy-duty kind the police used when they ran out of handcuffs. He wouldn't be able to break out of these without doing some serious damage to himself.

When he was sure he could speak calmly, Chuck said, "You've got me incapacitated. I couldn't identify you if I wanted to. Take whatever you want and leave."

The man pulled one of the overstuffed chairs next to the window over to the bed and sat down in it, crossing his legs at the knee and resting his arm so that the gun pointed at Chuck's head. "You're in no position to give orders. I suggest you tell me what I want to know, and your position will improve. Don't tell me what I want to know, and you won't have much time to be sorry about it."

The DA in Owings took over. He noted that the man was relatively articulate, probably educated beyond high school. The fact that he didn't have a noticeable accent suggested West Coast, maybe Far West. Chuck hadn't heard the voice before, but it was distinctive enough that he would recognize it again if he heard it.

He also guessed the man was a professional. His sweatsuit was black and a common brand. The ski mask was tight on his face and tucked into a turtleneck sweater. The gloves were belted tight at the wrist. The man's sweatpants were taped tight at the ankles. Even the gun was a common brand, a favorite among homeowners, criminals and cops. Whatever evidence he left behind him would be in threads, lint, or fiber. None of it would provide a DNA sample or any other speck of evidence to tie the man to this apartment.

"What kind of questions?" Chuck asked.

His first reaction was to believe this was someone

with a grudge against him, perhaps someone he had con-
victed, but that didn't seem likely. He would have recognized the voice. His second thought was someone had
been hired to kill him. If this were a pro, he would have
popped Chuck as soon as he walked in the door. Without
the questions the man wanted to ask, Chuck didn't have
a clue what he wanted.

"Where's the information you have on the Baker family?"

"The Bakers?" he asked, hardly keeping the incre-
dibility out of his voice. "You want to know about the
Bakers?"

The man patiently tapped the barrel of the gun on his
knee. "The Bakers," he said.

"I don't have anything about the Bakers. Pam Livingston down in Medford has most of the information
on them, and that writer who came in over a year ago.
When Pam and I broke up, I was out of the Baker
thing."

"No papers squirreled away in a safe-deposit box?"

"I don't even have a safe deposit box. Everything I
own is either here or in the office."

The tapping started again and then suddenly stopped.
"I've searched both of those, and I haven't found one
thing related to the Bakers."

"What do you mean you searched...?" The words
trailed off. Chuck thought it would be impossible for
someone to search his office. But then, he thought it
would be impossible for someone to get into his apartment. "How'd you get in my office?"

"I grew wings and flew. If you knew how I did it,
then I'd have to kill you."

"Please, don't bother to tell me."

Neither of them laughed.

"Tell me about the Baker estate."

"How much do you want to know? I have a date who's going to start missing me soon."

"I want to know about the money."

"Pam Livingston could tell you more—"

"Pam Livingston's not here."

This, Owings told himself, was not a person to try to bullshit. He searched his memory about the money. There was so much of it tied up so many ways, he wasn't sure what he could tell the man. "I don't remember exactly. I think Pam found six or seven million besides the funds set aside to preserve the estate. Every time she found some money, she was immediately confronted with paperwork that bound it back to the estate. That damn Kate Baker was brilliant when it came to keeping other people's hands off her money, even after she was long dead."

"And what about money that wasn't tied up by paperwork?"

"I don't know what you're talking about. We didn't find any money under floorboards or beneath mattresses. We only found it in banks, securely rooted there in paperwork that made it impossible to move it into anything but the Baker estate. Once we rounded it all up, we had millions earning ridiculously low interest rates because the will didn't allow us to invest it and knotted so tight we could only stand back and admire it from a distance. That's why Pam tried so hard to prove she was the legal heir to the money."

"And did she?"

"Yeah, right. Paul Fischer made sure she didn't do that."

"So you're saying that Pam Livingston has the papers

from the Baker estate, and you don't know any more than you told me?"

"Look, Pam dumped me. Even if there was a bundle of cash hidden away someplace, I'd be the last person on earth she'd want to share it with. I left Medford glad to get out of the Baker affairs and glad to get away with my reputation intact. I tell you, all that money was about to suck us both down into a pit."

The man sat silently for a moment, apparently pondering what questions he had not asked. He tapped the gun on his kneecap again, briefly, and then he seemed to sag in the chair a bit. Finally, he asked, "If I told you there was still more money, probably not in a bank, where do you think it would be?"

"Baker money?"

"Baker money."

"Jesus, I don't know. The only building left is the house. The only things besides that are the grounds, the creek that runs through it, the woods behind the house, and the pond. If anything was hidden any place else, it is either long gone or long ago found and disappeared. Pam and I searched the estate pretty thoroughly ourselves."

The man nodded his head. "I did the same."

Chuck kept himself from whistling in admiration. Getting on the estate undetected was difficult at best. Getting in the house undetected was almost impossible since they'd put the security cameras in.

"Why do I get the feeling that you know something I don't?"

The man stood up. "I appreciate your time," he said. "I assume your date will sound an alarm and someone will be checking on you." He disappeared from Chuck's view, silently.

Chuck strained to hear which way the man went to get an idea of how he had gotten into the apartment. As soon as he was sure the man was gone, he'd roll off the bed and over to the wall. On his back he could lift his legs to bang his feet on his neighbor's wall. The guy was usually home this time of the evening.

He doubted if he could get help in time to get the cops here to catch the guy, but if nothing else, he would get on the phone and call Pam. She needed to know that some nut was running loose with his eyes on the Baker fortune.

Something tickled the hairs on the back of his neck. He flinched a bit, and then it tickled the hairs again. Before he could figure out what it was, a bullet smashed into the base of his skull and stopped his thoughts forever.

The man in black waited just a few seconds to make sure that Chuck Owings was dead, and then he slipped from the bedroom. Sliding doors on the far side of the living room opened onto a terrace. Using a drainpipe like a rope, he lifted himself hand-over-hand up to the roof. From there he crossed to the back of the building and let himself down the fire escape he had used to get to the roof. Before he dropped down into the alley behind the building, he removed the ski mask, the gloves, and the tape around his sweat pants and tucked them into a fanny pack, along with the gun. He then jogged out of the alley, down the block to the corner, and across the street to the park, where he became just another runner getting in some exercise after a hard day at work.

NINE

PAUL STOOD IN Pam's backyard near two cedar trees connected by the hammock that hung between them, and stared off into the night sky, where the stars were brilliant gems of light a thousand fold. With the orchard on two sides of the property, the arborvitae separating the house from the neighbor's, and the street side of the land bordered by tall firs, there was little in the way of man-made light to distort the view to the stars.

The stars fascinated him. He could not grasp the distances between the stars and the depth of the universe. He only knew that on a clear night like this one, the earth became a very tiny spot in the heavens.

Tonight he thought about Kate Baker. He had lived her life for months, tracking her life from birth through childhood, and then into her adult years. Although he had briefly skimmed through later years, in his heart he left her in full womanhood, a victim of a difficult life poorly prepared for it by a family that only knew how to complicate living.

On this night, he stepped into her soul once again, as she stood on the front lawn of the Baker house where she too could stare off in the night sky and see the stars. Unlike his own vision, her vision would be clouded by tears. Tears for a family warping itself from the inside out. Tears for the dead man she still loved, the father of her child. Tears for the child she gave up. She was only thirty-two at that moment, but already her life was over. Others who might have seen the beautiful woman would have thought otherwise. She still turned heads when she walked the streets of Jacksonville and Medford. She still owned a huge ranch. She was very rich by the standards of the day. But, despite all of that, her life was over—over because she chose it to be.

Paul could not imagine it. He knew that her struggle to become a doctor, having to travel to France to have the opportunity to study for her medical degree, took a lot out of her. He knew that the war years when she practiced as a battlefield surgeon had nearly destroyed her, the final blow the death of Dr. Angelo Ferrano, the only man she'd loved. The only man she'd allowed in her bed.

She was too strong to give up on life as she had. Paul was almost disappointed in her because she seemed to quit trying to do any more than preserve the Baker wealth and fight off her sister's attempts to control it. Except, he knew her better than anyone. She had gotten the idea that the wealth was an evil thing that destroyed Bakers. That was why she had given up her son. She didn't want him destroyed by the wealth, too. Her mission in life from the time she was thirty-two on was to make sure that would not happen.

What was it he had read about Oliver Baker? Colonel Baker, "Colonel O" as he was called by the men who served with him, had told one of them about his childhood. He had said that he was drawn across the valley to the Baker Ranch as a child to catch a glimpse of the beautiful woman who still rode the land on horseback to supervise its operation. He said he had never seen such a beautiful woman, and he felt that they were somehow connected to each other.

Apparently he had added wryly that she hadn't felt the same way. Every time she spotted him on the ranch, she would send someone along to run him off. She never came herself. She would just sit tall in the saddle and watch him be led away until he disappeared from her sight. He couldn't ever remember her smiling. If she had, it would have broken his heart, he said.

His adoptive mother complained about the trips across the valley to the ranch. She said an eight-year-old had no business traveling all those miles. His adoptive father said the boy had to follow whatever it was that led him to the ranch.

Paul wondered if Kate would go back to her house and disappear into her room to cry whenever she saw the boy. He could not imagine Kate Baker, as strong as she could be, not letting the boy get to her. He was her son, more so because the Baker gene had overpowered Angelo's. Oliver was blond and blue-eyed, straight and strong like his mother.

And then Paul felt a longing for his own boys, so deep and so powerful that he was tempted to go into the cottage and call them, even though it would be after midnight on the East Coast. He had made a half turn, intent on doing just that, when headlights swept into the driveway, and he soon heard the purr of the big Mercedes.

The spell was broken. He walked toward the driveway and met Pam as she stopped the car and got out, still dressed for business in what his ex-wife called a power suit, and loaded down with a heavy briefcase.

"If you give me twenty minutes, I'll bring a bottle of wine and meet you on the deck."

As she walked away from him, he asked after her, "Do you ever think about your father?"

She stopped and looked back at him over her shoulder. "My real father? I never knew him. He died before I was born. What's there to think about him?" She didn't give him a chance to answer, disappearing quickly into the house and shutting the door a little more firmly behind her than perhaps she intended.

He doubted if she was telling the truth. Paul had thought about Oliver Baker a lot. He could not imagine Pam not doing the same. He walked back into the yard and climbed into the hammock. With hands behind his head, he stared again into the dark. If the massive night sky made the earth seem small to him, the Bakers made Paul feel even smaller. Their lives, like the stars, took on a glow of their own.

When Pam returned she was wearing blue slacks and a white, long-sleeved shirt with snap-down pocket flaps. She looked both elegant and country at the same time. He couldn't remember her wearing anything so informal in the months they'd known each other before. She had always been on guard with him, and her clothes had been her shield. When they had gone to bed and the clothes were gone, she still fought giving herself to him, but her body betrayed her. Perhaps, for a few moments in all of that, her heart had betrayed her as well. Something had sparked between them that went beyond the Baker fortune.

She carried a tray with a bottle of wine and two chilled glasses. She placed the tray on a patio table and poured two glasses before stepping on the lawn and bringing one to him. While he sat on the hammock, she pulled up a nearby lawn chair just a little out of his view, so he'd have to twist his head around if he wanted to see her. "This is an Oregon wine," she said. "Our wines are catching up with the world. We may someday be better known for them than our trees."

"I thought it was your rain you were known for."

"I've often laughed about that. We get about two-thirds less rain than Florida. We don't have the temperature extremes of the northern states, or the humidity of the southern states. We rarely get snow in our valleys. If anything, our temperatures are, on average, pretty moderate. Still, most people think of rain when they think of us."

"I don't," he said.

"I know what you think of. You think of your precious Kate Baker and how wronged you were by Nora, Chuck and me."

"You give yourself too much credit," he said, holding the glass of white wine high up to the sky to see if he could see the stars through it. He could, and the wine softened their glow just enough to turn them from diamonds to pearls. "I haven't thought about any of you much at all in the last year. If I hadn't noticed that the picture of Kate Baker had been taken from my office, I might not have thought about you again."

Her voice had just a bit of frost to it. "I guess I did give us too much credit."

"No, I wouldn't say that." He sipped the wine. It was a little dry, and a little sweet. All in all it wasn't bad. "You kept the wheels in my head spinning for nearly a year, and then the divorce from Beth and the need to find a job took over and you three got stored on a shelf full of old memories, good and bad."

"And Kate Baker?"

"I kept her picture on my desk for inspiration. She

was a remarkable, gifted woman who let life steamroll over her. I don't want to be steamrolled."

"Why did you ask about my father?"

He craned his neck a little to see her face, but she'd positioned herself away from the dim light coming from the house so he could see no more than the outline of her head. "When I was finishing up the book on Doc Hollingsworth, I ran across some information on Oliver Baker. I just wondered what you thought of him." Paul sensed her anger toward her real father, and he was curious about it.

He had succumbed to Pam Livingston's charms once before. He wasn't going to let it happen again unless he better understood her. A key to understanding the three sisters had been Oliver Baker. He suspected that Oliver Baker might be the key to understanding Pam.

"Old photos, newspaper clippings, and a box of medals don't mean anything to me. That's all I know of him. Mother told me that their marriage wasn't going very well when he went to Vietnam. If he hadn't died, she thought they might have been divorced."

He wondered what Kate Baker might have thought of that biography of her son. Flew planes. Won medals. Marriage failed. Got killed. This was the fate she had saved for him. "That's it? You don't have any other feelings?"

"Listen, Paul, when you get your license to be a shrink, I'll tell you about those feelings. But for now, you'll just have to settle for this: Jack Livingston married my mom. He adopted me. He was the only father I ever knew. He was good to me, treated me as his own. I've no complaints."

"But he certainly wasn't the romantic figure that Oliver Baker was. I would have thought an imaginative young girl would have had marvelous fantasies about a man like your real father.''

''He wasn't interested in being a father. He got himself killed.'' The frost turned to a sheet of ice. This was forbidden territory to explore.

''I never did run across any info about his remains. Where are they?''

''Mother told the military to dump them in the Gulf of Tonkin where he belonged.''

So the bitterness ran from mother to daughter. Or maybe it ran both ways. ''What did you want to talk to me about?''

''About Nora. About your break-ins. I'm concerned for my own safety.''

Paul thought about that. The man had gotten into the museum past a security system. He had broken into Paul's apartment and garage with ease. He had gone undetected in a secured building on campus under the nose of patrolling security guards. There was no telling where all he might have been. Pam had every reason to be concerned.

''I think,'' he said, ''without knowing what he's looking for, we can't know how seriously to take all of this. You haven't turned away any researchers lately, asking about the Bakers?''

''After you left, I wrapped up every loose end about the Bakers I could. If someone tried to write a biography about them from what's left, they'll have a very thin book indeed. Only you have any important information that I don't. If anyone has thought about writing another biography, they must have become so discouraged by how little information there is, that they gave up before they got to me.''

''That's a shame,'' I said. ''It's a good story.''

"If you're not a Baker."

He finished his glass of wine. "I've thought about it a lot since you called. Unless you have a hidden line of ancestors, no obvious connection pops to mind. My guess is both of us missed something in our research, something that someone else discovered."

"What could that be?"

"If someone is trying to find that out on both sides of the country, my best guess is it would have to do with money, and a lot of it. You don't go to this kind of trouble to write a nice biography about the Bakers when the two of us have locked away all the juicy stuff, things that no one else could know about."

"I can vouch for the fact that the will is iron-clad. If I couldn't get to the money, no one else is going to have a clearer track to it."

"That's why I think we missed something. As reluctant as I am to do it, I think I'll need to retrace my research into the sisters to see if I missed anything. I suggest you do the same thing."

She was quiet. When she spoke, the frost was gone from her voice, but a thinly disguised strain replaced it. "I'm not anxious to go through this again. I beat my head against a wall after you left, frustrating myself at every turn that led to a dead end. If it hadn't been for Nora, I would have let all of this slide."

He really wanted to believe her, but he also remembered how successfully they all had made a sucker of him the last time. Believing still wasn't easy. "If you want answers, you'll need to look. If there is something major in all this we overlooked, then both of us might be in a greater danger than we think."

Just then the phone in the house rang. Pam got up and walked across the lawn to the deck and then inside through the French doors. While she was gone, Paul slipped out of the hammock and went to the patio table to pour himself a little more wine.

He had just raised the glass to his lips when Pam walked stiffly back through the French doors. She wavered just a bit on her feet and then the wine glass slipped from her hand and broke on the deck. "Chuck Owings has been murdered," she said.

TEN

THEY SAT IN lawn chairs on the deck in the dark, sipping their glasses of wine, saying nothing to each other. What was there to think? Paul wondered. For him Chuck Owings was an abstract figure, a man he had met only a few times, and most of those had not been very pleasant. Chuck Owings had an agenda then that had conflicted with Paul's.

Paul relied on his initial impressions of Chuck when he had swept into Pam Livingston's office the first time Paul had met him. Paul had liked him. He brought into the office a power, an energy, and a sense of humor that transformed it for the few minutes he was there.

He could only imagine what Pam was thinking. The stem of a new wineglass revolved in her fingers. Her gaze traveled deep into the stars. The farther she looked into the night, the more she would see. Nearest was Chuck Owings, the district attorney who had been a match for her in the courtroom. A little deeper was Chuck Owings the lover. Paul had no illusions about that. The two had been engaged at one time, and they were both grown-ups. He couldn't see either one of them becoming engaged unless they were compatible in bed.

Deeper yet in the stars was Chuck Owings the co-conspirator. This may have been the one element of their relationship that bound them together. They both wanted

Kate's money. Pam wanted it because she believed it rightfully belonged to her. Paul did not know Chuck Owings well enough to know why he wanted it.

Before she broke her probe into the night, one solitary tear rolled down a cheek on Pam's face. She did not seem to notice it or she would have wiped it away, Paul thought. Pam Livingston was a very strong woman, one who would only have one tear for a man she once thought she loved.

PAUL SLEPT A restless sleep that night. Neither one of them had broached the subject, but it couldn't be too much below the surface. Had Chuck been killed by the same man who attacked Nora and broken into Paul's places? The only message Pam had been given was that Chuck had been murdered, and the Tacoma police wanted to talk with people who knew him to see if someone from Medford might have been carrying a grudge against him.

Pam and Paul agreed to meet for lunch. By the time he got out of bed, she was already gone. He made himself a cup of coffee and wandered out to the deck. There he found the morning newspaper neatly folded and left on the table for him. He stretched out on a lounge chair with his face to the sun and read the story on the front page, the one announcing Owings' death.

The story was short, obviously breaking shortly before this paper went to press. Owings had failed to show for a date. The woman, not one to be stood up, went to his apartment house. The security guard assured her that Owings had come in earlier and he had not seen him come out.

Because the woman demanded, and perhaps because she was probably quite attractive, the guard relented and took her to Owings' apartment. When ringing the bell got no answer, he let himself in to see if perhaps the district attorney had had an accident of some kind, had fallen asleep, or had forgotten about his date. That was when he found the body.

The article said little more than that. Most of the story was a recap of Owings' career in Medford. Details of how he was murdered were not included in the story.

Pam was already at the Mexican restaurant where they had agreed to meet. This was the same spot where they had eaten lunch the first time they had met. What a difference, he thought, as he sat down. In the beginning the playing field had not been level. The advantage went to Pam. Today the field was flat and they were beginning over again.

After he ordered for both of them, he asked, "Any more on Chuck?"

Her hair wasn't quite in place and her makeup wasn't quite right. Beyond that and the lack of expression on her face, he couldn't tell how much she was grieving. "There's no doubt he was murdered. He was found bound hand and foot on his bed with a single bullet to the back of the head."

"Any clues?"

"According to the Tacoma police, it was one of the cleanest hits they've seen. They don't know how the guy got in or got out. No one saw anything. They're getting almost nothing in the way of trace evidence, and what they have they can't say for sure came from the murderer. They think it might be a hired hit, but the gun seems to be wrong for a professional."

"I didn't know they had a preference."

"They do. They like a twenty-two-caliber gun. They're easy to come by, ammunition is plentiful, and they can be silenced to almost no noise at all. Anything bigger, despite what you see in the movies, makes a noise, silencer or no silencer.''

"What was this gun?''

"A nine-millimeter. They think it was an automatic. Unlike the twenty-two, which can be picked up cheaply, this is a more expensive gun. It's not the kind you toss away and feel good about. Kind of like setting some hundred dollar bills on fire.''

"What do you think?''

For a moment he thought the mask would crack and she would let out the tears. Instead she waited just a beat to stay composed and then said, ''I don't know. Chuck, like any DA, made his share of enemies. Dozens of bad guys have said they'd like to see him dead. But face it, neither Tacoma nor Medford are exactly the crime capitals of the world. If someone hired a hit, they'd have to have a good sum of money they wouldn't mind paying. I can't think of anyone with that kind of money who was mad enough at Chuck to have him killed.''

"Do you think it had anything to do with the Baker estate?''

She took a deep breath and held it. After she had eased it out, she said, ''I'm going to think it does until somebody proves me wrong. I don't want to end up with a bullet in the back of my head. Don't come knocking on my door late at night or you might get shot.''

Was she being melodramatic? Could this have anything to do with the other incidents? It did not seem likely. ''Are you sure you need to be that concerned?''

"I'm not sure of anything. He might have stepped on someone's toes in Washington. He might have been nosing into something no else knows about yet. Any number of things could have gotten him killed. They are pretty sure, though, that it was not a woman, and it was not a robbery. Those two and drugs are usually what get people killed.''

''No love triangles?''

She stared at him, the mask suddenly shattered by a flare of anger. ''Don't humor yourself. Chuck, you and I did not have a love triangle. His and my relationship was on hold when you and I went to bed, something like the relationship between you and your wife at the time. You needed me to know that you still needed to give your marriage more time. I needed you to know that Chuck wasn't the right one for me. We both got something valuable out of it beyond a romp in the hay.''

He held up his hands, trying to placate her. ''I wasn't even thinking about the three of us,'' he said. ''I just wanted to make sure Chuck wasn't sleeping with someone he shouldn't have been sleeping with.''

She calmed a bit. ''According to the people who knew him up there, he was having a great time on the singles scene. He didn't have to look much beyond his health club for new playmates. He certainly didn't have to look at women already attached to other men.''

''And Chuck wouldn't have been into drugs?''

''You might not believe this, but Chuck was a professional. He had an aggressive nature, and his favorite targets were the bad guys. He loved to put them in jail. He would have never done anything that would have jeopardized his career. He loved it too much.''

He nodded, but he remembered a time when Chuck Owings had held a gun on him, and a time when the DA had used his office to try to get information out of Paul for his own personal gain. In her grief, Pam was conveniently forgetting quite a lot about Owings.

''Okay,'' he said. ''We don't discount a connection

between his death and what has happened to Nora and to me. But why kill Chuck and not us?''

''Maybe he thought he had everything he needed from Chuck.''

He didn't like that answer. That suggested someone who was not just determined, but someone who was also ruthless. He didn't want to think about it. He hoped the Tacoma police would come up with a nice punk killer who wanted a notch on his gun for knocking off a DA. ''I guess we wait to see what the cops come up with.''

''I'm still keeping my door locked and a gun under my pillow.''

''No late night visits from me. You wouldn't have a spare gun, though, would you?''

For the first time she smiled. ''Yell loud and I'll come to your rescue.''

''You already rescued me once,'' he said. ''I was an emotional basket case when I came here the first time. My wife had rejected me for another woman. I was questioning my own self-worth. Going to bed with you did a lot to restore my ego, rightfully so or not. To be seduced by a beautiful woman hits at something primal in a man.''

''Don't give it more significance than it's worth. Mature adults get to go to bed with each other without it being more than mature adults going to bed with each other. At the time I remember enjoying it. It's nice not to have bad memories or feel like I need to kick myself for making a mistake. Beyond that, I chalk it up as just one more of those things we do on the journey of trying to find our way.''

Okay, he thought. She had no romantic notions about the past. That was fine. It also meant no undeserved recriminations.

She put her napkin down on the table. "I need to get back to work. You get to pay for lunch. I won't be home until late." As she got up, she thought to ask, "And what will you be doing today?"

"Watching my back, mostly."

"Besides that?"

"Start retracing some of the sources of information I used finding out about Hollingsworth and the Bakers. I might have overlooked something."

"I suppose you still have your original materials safely stowed away." She had a look on her face that struggled not to be condescending. She knew damned well he still had the materials carefully stowed away.

"No comment," he said.

"I thought so."

"And I assume your materials are well protected."

"You and an army division couldn't get to them."

"That's what you thought last time," he said, unable to resist the jab.

"If you get to these materials, you'll have broken a few federal laws."

"That means a bank and a safe-deposit box."

"No comment."

"That's what I'd do," he said.

She leaned over the table and kissed him lightly on the cheek. "No you wouldn't," she said, "not here, not when you went home, and not back in Maine."

"You know that, do you?"

"After you left the state, Chuck and I tracked your every move. The stuff you accumulated on the Bakers is still in this valley. If it hadn't been such a big valley, I would have bought a shovel and started digging."

He had a thought. "You didn't buy the house on

Shady Lane because you thought I might have left something behind there, did you?''

"I bought the house because I love it.''

"No other reason?''

"Okay, so I searched one end of the property to the
other. I would have bought the house anyway.''

He believed her about the house. It was a find. As
isolated as it was, it was only a few miles from both
downtown Medford and California Street in Jacksonville, Doc Hollingsworth's home.

"I'm sorry if I disappointed you.''

"It wasn't a complete waste. I found one of your
socks under the agitator in the washing machine, and I
found a dollar thirty-five in change under the cushions
of the sofa.''

"You found my treasures.''

"Yeah, but I didn't find mine. I'll see you this evening.''

He watched her walk away, a handsome woman followed by a dozen eyes in the restaurant, some belonging
to men and the others to women. He wondered what they
were thinking. The men, he imagined, would be admiring her as a supreme example of her species. Women,
on the other hand, might be thinking catty thoughts. *A
woman like that*, he imagined them thinking, *makes all
the rest of us look bad.*

Paul shrugged to himself. Women were women. He
wasn't much of an expert on them, and that was one of
the reasons he'd been so fascinated by the lives of the
Baker sisters. He learned a lot about women in general
from the three of them.

He paid for the meal and left the restaurant, catching
himself smiling when he sighted the Alfa sitting in the
parking lot with its top down. If he was a man who
desperately wanted to be locked in the ivory tower of

academics behind vine-covered walls, why did he get such a kick driving around in the sunshine with the top down on the sports car? Maybe the one thing he knew the least about, other than women, was himself.

He started up the car, listened to its nice little purr for a moment, and then pulled out of the parking lot, nosing into traffic that would take him out of town, back to Shady Lane, and beyond. Yes, he was up to his old tricks again. In the trunk of the car was a length of rope and a few other tools, just in case he needed them. He was ready to visit the sisters again, and maybe break into their Victorian masterpiece once again, just for old-time's sake. If Pam knew what he was about to do, she might have given him the key, but that would have taken all the fun out of it.

Paul had to search a little longer this time to find the access road that led to the bottom of the slope on which sat the Baker house. A new subdivision had gone in, gobbling up more of what had been the Baker Ranch. Kate had divested the estate of much of its land before she died, donating most of the money to public schools, universities that supported women's studies, hospitals, and charities. She had been in a hurry to spend the Baker fortune before her death. She had failed. Pam had located stocks, bonds, large quantities of cash, and even gold bars scattered around the valley in different banks. It added up to a considerable fortune, all which could not be touched legally except to preserve the Victorian mansion and the surrounding grounds.

He stopped the Alfa on the dirt road next to the forty-foot wall that had been built to protect the shelf on which the house sat. A four-foot iron fence was located along the edge of the front lawn, each eight-inch-spaced bar topped with an ornate spearhead.

Paul pulled out a coil of rope from the trunk of the car, making a loop at one end, and then heaved it up the wall. He managed to catch one of the spearheads on the third try. Once convinced that the rope was secure, he put on a pair of leather gloves he'd purchased along with the rope. He pulled himself up the rope slowly, hand over hand. He wasn't in as good shape as the last time he'd done this, so by the time he reached the top, he was glad to hang from two bars in the fence by his hands for a minute or more until he caught his breath.

He pulled himself over the fence, delicately, because he was mindful of the sharp tips of each of the spears. Finally he stood on a spot of ground to which he thought he would never return. To his left were the graves of the sisters and their parents, and to his right was the road that led up to the house from behind it. A high fence that was monitored by sensors and cameras surrounded the grounds of the estate. To get in through the gates, a person would need a key to a box that allowed the person to punch in a security code to disarm the alarms.

He knew, too, that the doors and windows of the house all had sensors on them, and the house itself was monitored internally by cameras that recorded movement and sent out an alarm. Pam had made it clear to him that he would not get back in the house again without being detected. He suspected that she hoped he had left his research material hidden somewhere in the house, and, if she could keep him out of it, then it would only be a matter of time before she found it for herself.

That was good thinking on her part, but, of course, that wasn't where he'd hidden it. He walked over to the graveyard, surrounded by its own iron fence with spear-tipped bars, one not as high as the fence across the front of the property. It was here, in front of Kate Baker's headstone, that he had buried the research material. He wasn't here for it, at least not yet. He needed to know more about the mysterious man who seemed to be seeking out information on the Bakers before he dug it up. The last thing he wanted to do was reunite himself with it, only to have it taken away from him.

No, he came up here to gaze on Kate Baker's grave and to examine just exactly what it was he felt about her now. When he first saw her portrait in the Jacksonville museum, he'd been swept off his feet by her. She had led him through an exhilarating journey, traveling with the Bakers as they struggled through life. He had admired her, he had been in awe of her, and he had even loved her. More than once he had ached because he had been born generations too late and that she, an older woman, had died before he was born. He would have loved to have met her just once, to have heard her voice. He was sure he would not have been disappointed.

He walked to the slope and stood with his hands on the fence, staring across the valley. Few homes anywhere in the Rogue River Valley had a view as good as this one. How many times had he imagined Kate standing here and seeing the same view he was enjoying? Yes, much had changed; the fine lines of the valley were etched in more detail now, but the golden hills to the southeast were the same shape, the timber still disappeared over the rises to the west, and the two of them still came together near Ashland in the south. The sky was every bit as blue today as it had been when she was alive. The air still smelled of sun-baked grasses and baked fruits and baked foliage, much like it would have smelled for her.

What had she thought, he wondered, when she'd stood here to take in the sensuous feast? What were her thoughts when her life was nearing its end? What was it that she had done, somewhere in all of that, which suddenly attracted the interest of a shadowy figure who was willing to harm an old lady, to break in and steal, and maybe even to commit murder to find out?

He would feel a lot better if he knew for sure who had killed Chuck Owings. He wanted that person to be someone who had nothing to do with the Bakers.

A flash of light caught his attention. In the distance, on the highway near where he had entered the dirt road, he could just make out a car parked on the side of the road. Someone seemed to be leaning over the roof of the car, staring at him. He squinted against the glare of the sun. Yes, someone seemed to be watching him with binoculars.

Paul was curious. He climbed over the fence and lowered himself back to the road below. He then flicked the rope a number of times until the loop came loose. He wound it quickly and threw it on the passenger seat before he jumped in, started the car, and raced it back to the highway. He was suddenly very curious to know who it was with the field glasses.

He skidded the Alfa to a stop at the end of the dirt road. There, in front of him on the highway, was an empty spot where the car had been. He pulled out on the asphalt and looked both ways. No car was in sight in either direction. Whoever it was had left in a hurry, leaving behind two rubber patches on the road.

ELEVEN

NORA RYAN LIVED in fear. She had always been a woman who got what she wanted from life, in marriage, in a career, and in recognition for her strength of character. She wanted to be a woman who was admired and respected, but also one who made people a little uncomfortable, especially men.

She had made that work for her successfully for a number of years. When she was appointed curator of the Jacksonville Museum, it was after she had gone head-to-head with applicants from as far away as Kansas City, Missouri. She got the job in part because she was the best candidate, but also because her character intimidated enough members of the selection board that they were afraid not to hire her.

In truth, she had been a good pick. She had developed the children's museum next to the Jacksonville Museum, she had opened a storefront branch of the museum in Medford that tantalized enough to draw visitors to Jacksonville, she had rotated the displays frequently with a theme in mind, and then she had advertised the changes on television, on radio, and in the press. She even had her own weekly cable television and radio shows on the history of southern Oregon.

Or at least she'd had those shows before the beating. The radio show had been canceled. The television program had been taken over by the history department at the college in Ashland. Nora and other department members had worked together often enough to produce other shows, so that it was only natural that they step in.

All had changed that night not so much because of the physical damage done to her, which had been brutal enough, but because of the psychological damage. She had led a charmed life with few defeats. No man had dared to threaten her physically because she was so strong, so dominant. She had even begun to believe it herself. Until that night.

When she finally came out of the coma, when she finally fought through the natural instinct to block the memory of the attack, and when she finally confronted the terror of that moment, something inside of her broke. Call it will, call it spirit, call it whatever, once it was gone, much of what had made Nora Ryan who she was, was gone as well.

She was now a frightened woman. She was a woman who hid in her house with the curtains closed and the doors locked, one who had a gun in her bed stand and another one in her purse. She was a woman who was devastated, afraid of she knew not what. Like Pam Livingston, like Paul Fischer, even like Chuck Owings, she did not have a clue what this was about.

She had waded through it in her mind over and over again. She knew as much about the Bakers as anyone, even more than Paul Fischer suspected. Yet, even with this knowledge, she couldn't think of a single reason why someone would want to steal the information about the Bakers. There was nothing to be learned about the Bakers that could benefit anyone but Pam Livingston.

She sat in a rocking chair in her living room and stared at the blank screen on the television. In the shiny reflection she hoped to see what it was that was the missing piece, the one thing that would tell her what this was all about.

If she had leaned back just a little in the chair and tilted her head slightly to the right, she would have seen in that reflection the man dressed in black quietly slipping up behind her. But because she didn't, she didn't know he was there until the barrel of his gun pressed against the side of her head and the man behind her appeared on the TV screen.

She was transfixed by the reflection on the television screen, immobile, paralyzed by her fear. Yet she was not immobile. It seemed like everything inside of her had leaped into motion, to the rhythm of her frantically beating heart, and only her body didn't move.

A soft whisper reached her, finally. "Don't come crashing down on me now, Nora."

She could not speak; she could not move. She could feel the gun barrel resting on the side of her head. She could sense the nearness of the man with the gun.

"What do you want?"

"You'll have to speak up, Nora. I can't understand your whisper."

She gathered herself up to force out the words again. "What do you want?"

"Not, 'Who are you?'" he asked, something in his voice mocking her.

"I know who you are. You're the one from the museum."

"Are you so sure of that?"

"Yes. The smell."

"Very good. Yes, the smell. I hadn't thought of that. That's very clever of you. I'll make sure to do something about that. You have an odor, too, that of a frightened old lady who just peed in her pants.''

"I guess I have a right."

He laughed softly. "Is a bit of that spunk of yours returning? I hadn't meant to beat it out of you."

She closed her eyes, hoping to erase this nightmare when she opened them. But she hadn't. He was still there in the reflection, a man dressed in black with a ski mask over his head, still pointing the gun at her head.

"What do you want?" she asked again.

"I want you tell me about the Bakers."

"All you need to know is in the material you stole."

"Let's call it borrowed. If you are good, you might just get it all back someday; in fact, you might even get to stay alive. What you gave me is not what I want to know. Now, I want to know the names of everyone else who has done any research on the Bakers."

"That's probably a dozen people."

"I'm listening."

She spent perhaps a half an hour narrating the attempts by various people to write about the Bakers, including her own. She told him what she knew about the information that Pam Livingston had about the Bakers. She ended her recount with Paul Fischer's research, the one, she said, who got further than any of them.

Nothing she said seemed to have any impact on the man in the reflection. He listened without visible sign as to what all of this meant to him. She had thought he'd ask about Fischer, but he didn't.

When she was finished, she asked, "Now what?"

"Now," he said, "you open your shades, you get a good night's rest, and you report back to work. While you're there, doing your usual admirable job of running the museum, you'll pick up your research on the Bakers, write up a complete report on what the others accomplished, and wait to hear from me again.''

"I can't pick up my research," she said. "You have it."

"Actually, I don't. It's all in a neat little package sitting on your desk at the museum. He ran the barrel of the gun gently up and down the side of Nora's face. "Don't think of calling the police, even your neighbor across the street. You should know by now that I come and go as I like. We all have remarkable little talents. Mine is to get into places others try so very hard to keep people like me out of. The house on the hill, the museum, your own house. My talents haven't even been remotely challenged. If you do as I tell you, your life will be given back to you. In the meantime, your life belongs to me. I'll be in touch.''

His image slipped from the television screen. If she hadn't watched him go, she would have sworn he was still there. He had not made a sound.

She sat for maybe an hour, and then she cautiously got up and walked through the house, turning on every light. When she was done, she could find no sign of him—and even more frightening, she couldn't find out how he had gotten in.

She never gave what she would do a second thought. She went to her closet and laid out clothes for work. The Bakers had already put her through a lot. What was one more thing?

TWELVE

PAUL SAT IN the dark in the guest cottage and listened to a tape of Gordon Lightfoot songs. He remembered back, years before, when he and Beth had gone to see the singer in concert. Lightfoot had nursed a fifth of whiskey on stage and had become belligerent as the evening went on. At one point he had refused to sing a song called out by someone in the audience because he said it was a "fag song." At another point, he had stopped in the middle of a song to shout at someone running the soundboard in the back of the theater. He yelled, "Turn the goddamn thing up or turn the goddamn thing down, but leave the goddamn thing alone."

Paul had left the concert feeling cheated. The music had been as good as he'd expected it to be; the man singing the songs was not. Perhaps that was why he had been so impressed with Kate Baker. He was never disappointed with each new thing he learned about her. She had a clear vision: The Baker wealth was their curse, so she got rid of it.

He wondered, if she could have looked ahead to the lives of Oliver and then Pam, if she would do the same thing today.

He had done one other task when he'd visited the house on the hill: He had stepped away from the bluff long enough to enter the grave site. There he had knelt at the head of Kate's grave and brushed some debris from the marker with her name on it. While he knelt there, he carefully unfolded a length of stiff wire he had carried in his pocket. When it was straight, he eased it into the soil between his knees and worked it in the ground. When it stopped, more than a foot below the surface, he ran it up and down several times until he was sure he'd hit the plastic box. The diaries and the disks on which he had the story of the Baker sisters were still there.

Unless something came up, he would have to dig up the box to get to the diaries. If he had overlooked something, it would be in one of those. He had not read them through carefully at the time. When the sisters moved into middle age, he'd begun to lose some of his interest. Most of what he remembered about that time was the squabbling between them.

Elizabeth was just generally cantankerous as the syphilis she had contracted from Rodney Ryan had returned to haunt her remaining days. Emily groused about the loss of Oliver to Uncle Tim. Kate, in a much more dignified way, complained about her sisters' complete lack of understanding.

He walked into the kitchen with the lights still out and poured himself a small amount of apricot brandy from a bottle on the table, seeing by the light that drifted through the window from a floodlight above the garage. He had purchased the brandy for himself. He wasn't a drinking man by nature, but returning to this valley made him want to drink.

He could look out through the orchard on the west side of the property from the table at the corner windows of the kitchen. Tonight, a misty rain fell that soaked everything through, so what he saw was not so much the trees, but thousands of glistening little jewels, the reflection of the floodlight off droplets of rain.

He wondered if the man who had watched him with the binoculars was out there someplace, still watching. If he was, he was probably pretty wet by now. Paul did not smile at the thought. He knew what the remains of the Baker fortune had done to Chuck Owings, Nora Ryan, and Pam Livingston. There was one moment when he thought Chuck Owings might kill him, and he might have if Pam hadn't stopped him. He never doubted for a moment that another person could be driven to the edge as had been those three.

Now he did smile to himself. He was paranoid; he just lacked an honorable reason for it. He had seen Pam briefly that evening when she came home from work. At her request, he had walked around the outside of her house to make sure each floodlight came on, the ones activated by motion sensors.

She had a complete security system inside the house, connected to a monitoring service. All doors had dead bolts and were chained. The windows were securely locked on the inside, armed with sensors, and protected on the outside by storm windows screwed tightly into place. As long as she stayed in the house, she remained in a fortress. But there was little to protect her once she stepped outside the house. He guessed that was why he was here. Her only request of him for staying in the cottage was that he be there when she got home, and he didn't leave before she did.

He had dressed in dark clothing earlier in the evening. For a reason. He set his glass on the table. He walked back through the living room and down a hallway that separated the bathroom from the bedroom and led to a back door. He slid the dead bolt back very quietly, dropped the chain, opened the door a crack and listened. He stood very still for nearly five minutes. Then, silently, he slipped out the back door.

He placed a single strand of straw, pulled from the broom in the kitchen, near the door handle, and then squeezed it between the door and the jamb. If someone opened the door before he returned, he would know it.

He moved slowly along the deep shadows of the house, and then swung out into the darkness behind it, making sure not to be caught by the floodlight. If nothing else, he'd learned stealth when he was in the valley last time.

Paul moved to the orchard on the south side of the property and disappeared into it, a half a dozen rows or so. Someone would approach the house from here, because the cottage would keep anyone in the house from seeing him. For the same reason, the person wouldn't stay here. He would need to be in the west orchard in order to see the house.

Paul was also sure the man would not approach from the lane to the north, or from the neighbors' side. A stranger walking down the lane or a strange car parked on the side of the road would be too obvious. The neighbor had a dog chained outside. No, if someone was out there, Paul knew about where he would be.

This might be the stunt of a fool or an idiot, but Paul didn't consider himself to be either one. He simply wasn't one to let a threat come to him. He would go to the threat first. Not unarmed, either. He slipped a .32 automatic pistol from his hip pocket and eased off the safety. He let the gun hang loosely by his right leg, but very much to the ready. Pam had given him the gun, one of several she had in her house.

He circled even deeper into the trees, moving very

slowly, not so much afraid he would make noise, but because he wanted to avoid walking into tree branches. The ground itself was freshly plowed and slightly damp. He made no noise at all as he walked.

He was more than twenty rows deep when he began working his way back to the house from the west. He moved up one row at a time, stopping at each one and rapidly scanning the trees ahead for even the slightest bit of movement. Then he examined each shadow that he could see, probing it, looking for even the remotest sign that it might hide a human.

The floodlights made the job easier by outlining the shadows ahead of him. The closer he got to the yard, the longer Paul scanned the shadows. His caution paid off. He was only two rows back and two rows to the left of the figure when Paul saw him. The man had nestled himself in close to the trunk of a tree, so well that he was almost indistinguishable from the shadow of the tree itself, except for the roundness of his head, which stood out clearly even among the branches.

Paul hesitated. He wasn't afraid. He had the gun and he was pretty sure he would use it if he had to, but he wasn't quite sure what to do. He could fire a shot to scare the man off, but then he might have a lot of explaining to do, like to the police. He could try to sneak up on the man and take him by surprise, something that usually worked well in the movies, but might lead to a shoot-out here in the trees, and that probably wouldn't do either of them any good.

Something cracked near Paul's head and bits of twigs slapped into his face. He dropped to the ground and rolled over and over into the deepest shadows he could find. He brushed his face with his free hand, and then, when he could focus clearly, he sighted his gun on the tree where the man stood. Had stood. He was gone.

Paul scanned the area around him, rolling onto his back to see behind him, and then rolling away again to another shadow. He pulled himself into a crouch, then made a quick dash to his left, running quickly through the trees to the lane. He didn't turn right toward the house. Instead, he turned left and walked in the shadows, along the edge of the orchard, until he was thirty or forty rows back.

Once again he entered the trees, moving cautiously in the darkness all the way back around until he entered the yard behind the cottage. It took him quite a bit of time, because he paused along the way dozens of time to scan the territory ahead of him. He didn't expect the man to still be in the orchard, but he wasn't going to be surprised again.

The straw was still wedged in the door. He let himself back inside, again quietly, silently slipping the chain and dead bolt back on while listening to the sounds of the cottage. Still not satisfied, he systematically searched each room, the gun in his hand leading the way. He finished the search in the kitchen, where he poured himself a much larger glass of brandy.

He needed it. He had seen the flash. He knew it was a shot fired from a gun with a silencer on it, and he knew the bullet had come dangerously close to his head, so close that his face had been stung by bits of the branch it had shattered.

It wasn't until he was safely again in the chair in the living room, this time sitting in silence with his glass of brandy, that he felt the fear. He'd been overmatched. The floodlight from the garage probably picked up enough of him for the man to make him out. That he had thought to look behind him suggested someone very cautious indeed.

What Paul didn't know about was the shot itself. Had the shooter just missed Paul because he had pulled the shot from his own inexperience or his own fear, or had he missed Paul because he hadn't wanted to kill him? If he had wanted to, he could have played a cat-and-mouse game with Paul and more than likely hunted him down. He chose to leave and avoid more of a confrontation.

Paul decided he'd try to follow the man's tracks in daylight and see where they led. The ground was soft and wet. That shouldn't be a problem. The greater problem, Paul now realized, was that he was no closer to understanding this than he had been before. The only difference now was that he was more frightened than he had been.

He slept in an overstuffed chair in the living room with his feet on the coffee table. Twice he woke up in the night and wandered the house, staring out into the yard from each of the windows, trying to see if the man had returned. He wouldn't expect him to. Both now knew this game they played.

The rules to the game were fascinating. They included traveling across country to steal from Paul. They included returning to steal from Nora and then beat her up. Did they also include killing Chuck Owings? The committee was still out on that rule, but the decision on it would certainly change the game.

HE GOT UP WITH the light, less stiff than he thought he would be, mainly because of the softness of the chair. He left the cottage through the front door this time, making sure the door was locked behind him.

He stopped first where he'd been standing when the

shot was fired at him. He found the exact spot marked by deep indentations in the soil where his feet had been when he'd hurled himself to the ground. He stood again in those indentations, easily finding the area in the tree where the twigs had been shattered. Just behind that spot was a thicker branch with a groove that crossed it. By lining up his head, the twigs, and the groove, he had an exact sighting to the position the man had held. He knew from the angle that the man must have held the gun shoulder-high, sighting along its barrel, before he fired, and he knew from all the angles that the bullet had passed by his head only an inch or two away.

He moved to the trunk of the tree where the man had stood. Looking back, he could see that the shot had been pretty spectacular, threading its way through foliage and branches to nearly hit its mark. He examined the area. He wasn't a cop nor a lab technician, but he was pretty sure few clues had been left behind. There were no candy wrappers or cigarette butts. Under close examination, he could not see an obvious fiber clinging to the trunk of the tree or nearby branches. That didn't mean a good technician wouldn't, but a good technician would only have been out here if the bullet had hit its mark.

He thought about the bullet. Lining up all the marks again, he could guess the path it took through the orchard. It might have caught the trunk of a tree farther on, but from the looks of it, the bullet was probably embedded in the soft dirt, rows away. He would look later, but he didn't expect to find it.

He then began to track footprints. He stopped once to stand by a pair, and then stepped out of his own prints to make a comparison. The man had bigger feet, and it was Paul's impression that he was a larger man. The other footprints were also deeper in the soil. He weighed more than Paul. A big man, with good night vision, and quick on his feet.

The footprints leading away from the tree showed no sign of panic. They were spaced a little broader than those coming toward the house, but not that much more. The man had not sprinted away; he had moved away in more of a jog.

He followed the footprints through the orchard to the spot where they crossed over his own and then to a road to the south. Here Paul found where the car had been parked. It was a bend in the road, next to a small bridge that crossed the road over an irrigation ditch. Because of the bend, the spot was out of view of houses on either side of the bridge.

He walked back to a spot that had confused him. The tracks had turned right, as if the man had not gone back to his car right away. Paul followed this set of tracks. Later, when he finally figured it out, he almost wished he hadn't. The man had circled back, much as Paul had done after he ran from the shot, only a little deeper into the orchard. Eventually the footprints had stopped and then doubled back on themselves. It was clear to see why. His tracks paralleled Paul's back through the trees. While Paul was moving deep through the orchard back toward the cottage, the other man had out-flanked him and followed him step for step, no more than thirty feet away the whole time.

Paul walked out of the trees to the back door of the cottage, and then he turned around and looked back into the trees. The man had followed him this far last night, stopping behind a tree until Paul had let himself into the cottage. And then the tracks moved from behind the tree onto the lawn where he had left enough of a trail of mud for Paul to know he had walked right up to the cottage, probably to stare into one of the windows to see what Paul was doing. Paul had been having a stiff drink at the time. He let himself in the back door and walked into the kitchen to pour another stiff drink.

THIRTEEN

THE BAKERS WENT TO quite a bit of trouble to protect the assets of the ranch. Kate, before she died, the only legal survivor of the estate, did her best to wrap up what was left of it from any desperate hands that tried to claim the fortune. For that reason alone, Paul was at a complete loss as to what this was all about. If Pam Livingston, the only person with a legitimate claim, couldn't crack the will, then what was there in it for anyone else? What could this man possibly want?

The sun was out again, and the morning was warm and bright. He was sitting on the deck drinking a cup of coffee when the French doors opened and Pam came out wearing a nightgown and carrying her own cup of coffee. She sat at the patio table across from him. "I had a wonderful night's sleep," she said. "The first one in a long time."

He struggled with what he should tell her. That he had played hide-and-seek with a man dressed in black in the middle of the night in the dark of the orchard? That the man had taken a shot at him, and the gun must have had a silencer on it, explaining why Pam's wonderful sleep hadn't been disturbed? That they were both up to their navels in something unpleasant, but he didn't have a clue what it was?

He considered telling her all of this, but then he decided not to. Let her have a few more good nights of sleep. She lived in a fortress, and for now she had him as a guard dog. Telling her right now wouldn't answer any questions. In fact, he might have a better chance of getting the answers if she didn't know.

"You obviously didn't sleep as well," she said.

He hadn't looked in the mirror this morning, but if being scared witless counted for anything, he had a right not to look like he had slept. "It was one of those nights," he said. "I must have had a cup of coffee too close to bedtime. I had a tough time staying asleep."

She seemed to accept what he said at face value. She moved directly to what was on her mind. "I'm flying to Tacoma this afternoon. Chuck's funeral is tomorrow morning. I'll be back in the evening."

"Will you need a ride to the airport?" he asked.

"No. I'll be going up with some other people who worked with Chuck. We've chartered an airplane. I'll get a ride with one of them."

He watched her face, looking for a clue there about her feelings for Chuck Owings. If what she told him was true, she had not gone back to Chuck after Paul. She must have had other men since him, other relationships that would have blunted her feelings for Chuck.

He couldn't imagine her not having other men. She was, short hair or not, still a gorgeous woman, no longer Kate Baker, but perhaps something better: a modern woman not held back by convention, who could wear her hair the way she wanted, and who was full of promise instead of defeat. He had been given a taste of her sexual appetite. No, there had to be other men. She was too much of a woman for that not to happen.

Why did that disappoint him? He and Beth had tried counseling. They'd even made it back to bed once or twice before it was obvious to both of them that it was over. And then there had been his neighbor. He hadn't exactly been chaste, and neither he nor Pam expected to see each other again. So why did it disappoint him?

"You can't stare at me forever without saying anything."

He focused and then saw the amused smile on her lips. He looked down at his coffee. "I'm sorry," he said. "Sometimes time gets jumbled and I'm coming my going."

She laughed. "Coming your going?"

He shook his head. "I'm not sure what it means, either, but I know how it feels."

"You want something. What is it?"

She had cut through something he had yet to cut through himself. Yes, he did want something. It wasn't her. Not yet. It was something else. "I want to stay in the house while you are gone," he said.

"My house?"

"Kate's house."

Her smile turned into an open-mouthed stare. Now it was her turn to try to read the expression on his face. He wondered if her search took her back to their time in bed. "Why?" she asked, finally.

"I've spent a good part of the night picking my brain. I can't for the life of me figure out what this is all about. Maybe a night in the house will give me a clue."

Did that sound as lame to her as it did to him? But what was he to say? "I need to create a diversion"? "I need to give the man in black an excuse to stay here with me and not follow you to Tacoma"? "I'm afraid what he might do to you when he does get to you. And I'm pretty confident that he will get to you in time"?

That's what he wanted to say, but he didn't dare because it sounded ridiculous even to him. Without knowing more, all he could do was imagine. Having a vivid imagination was hell. Getting shot at didn't help, either.

"You've hidden something up there, haven't you?"

The last time he was here he'd developed the remarkable ability not to look startled when she asked him questions like this. "I've been away from all of this for awhile. I've spent my time in the last year wondering if it was me or if it was my students who were the morons when they didn't do well on a test. If I stay in the house, a lot of the Baker story will come back to me. It might trigger an idea about this attacker." It would also leave him alone at an isolated spot with a man with a predilection for violence, which could well get him killed, but he decided not to add that.

"I think you're lying to me."

"I've got the diaries of the sisters hidden up there and I want to get back to them," he said, straight face and all.

She laughed so hard she nearly spilled the coffee from the cup resting in her lap. When she could, she said, "Like hell you do. The last time Chuck and I spent any time together was at the house turning it upside down from one end to the other, trying to find the diaries. I even had the safe opened, legally, as the guardian of the estate, to determine if anything might have been removed from it. You did not leave the diaries up there. I'm not even convinced now that there were diaries. I think if you removed anything from the safe it was financial records."

She was wrong, of course. Through a little masterful and incredibly lucky detective work, he had gotten the combination from the safe and taken from it the only three articles inside, the three sisters' diaries. "Okay, financial records," he said.

Pam shook her head no. "There's something else."

"I want to steal all the antiques."

She shook her head no again, laughing. "That's not it."

"I'm doing a research project on Victorian wallpaper."

Still laughing, she said, "You're not going to tell me, are you?"

"Can I stay in the house?"

She quieted quickly and sat silent for more than a minute. At last she said, "I'll let you in myself. I'll show you how to set the security system once you're inside, and how to turn it off, but I won't leave the perimeter system unarmed. That means no one else gets in after I leave. If you want to leave, you'll have to call the security company and have them come let you out."

He considered all of that. He wondered if she might be trying to protect him from the man in black, or if she was simply trying to protect her interest in the Baker estate.

"You mean I won't get to have a moving van come in after you leave?"

"Nor will you be able to rush out for a hamburger. You'll need to take along everything you'll need for two days."

"I sure hope your plane isn't delayed. I could starve to death up there."

"I'll have security come in on the morning after next to let you out and lock up the place should I not get back right away."

"Why are you letting me go?" he asked.

"Why do you need to go?" she snapped back.

A stand-off. They'd work together, but neither one of them was quite ready to fully trust the other. If that kept the man in black in the Rogue River Valley (by its name a place where he deserved to be), then he would leave it at that.

Apparently convinced that he wasn't going to answer her question, Pam got up, set her coffee cup on the table, and walked to the edge of the deck to stretch out her arms to the sunshine. He glanced back at her and then got that mule-kick in the stomach, that painful feeling a man gets when he sees a woman so desirable his system can't take it all at once. The bright sun made her thin gown almost transparent, and for a second, he couldn't imagine why he hadn't given her everything she wanted the first time they'd met.

TWO HOURS LATER he was carrying a box of groceries from Pam's car to the Baker house. He left the Alfa in the garage on Shady Lane, deciding he didn't really need it. If he wanted to leave, he could ride out with the security people when they came to lock up the place.

Pam gave him some quick instructions. A control panel that set the alarm system was in the entrance, near the front door. Pam had spent a large chunk of the Baker money on security after Paul had gotten inside the house so easily before. Paul could fully arm the house from the panel, and turn on the security cameras, motion detectors and door and window sensors.

She gave him the codes he needed, assuring him she'd have them changed once she returned. Since he wouldn't want the motion sensors on, she showed him how to turn them off for the whole house or particular areas. She had arranged the security that way in case she needed to have a repairman in. She could disarm the part of the house the repairman was in but leave the rest monitored. That way she didn't have to wait around for the work to be done.

The security cameras could be turned off at the panel as well, which meant the signal was not being sent back to the security monitoring service. She showed him an antique hutch in the den that had not been there before. In it were a half a dozen monitors; from here, he could monitor the house and the grounds by switching from one camera to the next, recording anything he saw if he felt like it.

Out of curiosity he asked, "Are these cameras on all the time?"

"No," she said. "The ones in the house are wired to the motion sensors. They go on if something is moving around inside. The cameras outside go on only if someone triggers one of the alarms. No one wants to handle eight cameras shooting twenty-four hours of tape every day. I'd have to hire someone full time just to replace the tapes."

So his trip to the house had not been noticed. If it had been, he was sure she would never have agreed to let him stay for the night.

She kissed him on the lips, a kiss that lingered just a bit. He had held her lightly, resisting the urge to pull her to him. As she drove off, he walked to the fence along the slope. Without surprise he noted the car in the distance, the man again leaning over the top with his binoculars aimed at him. Paul lifted a hand and waved. The other man did not respond.

After a few more minutes, the man lowered the binoculars and got into his car. He waited there for perhaps five more minutes, and then the car accelerated away. Paul watched as he worked his way back to the main highway, disappearing behind houses to emerge eventually at the intersection of the housing development and the road.

The driver stopped the car, and Pam passed him. After a few seconds, he turned onto the highway and followed the Mercedes, well back. Paul had warned Pam that she needed to be careful, that she needed to think of herself as always being followed. He wasn't concerned at the moment. She was driving directly to the airport where she would meet with the others; several of them who were cops. She would be safe for now. The only question was whether or not the man would come back.

Paul didn't waste any time. He went back in the house, made sure all the security cameras were turned off, and then pulled a small trowel and a folded piece of plastic out of his travel bag. In minutes he was kneeling at Kate Baker's headstone, carefully cutting a square of grass on three sides and then rolling it back to the uncut side, trimming the grass roots underneath as he went so that he could return it all intact. He then began to dig, putting the dirt on the unfolded sheet of plastic. Twenty minutes later he pulled the plastic box from the hole, and took out the computer disks and the three diaries. When he had what he wanted, he reburied the plastic box and rolled back the grass. Once he'd cleaned up his mess, he went back to the spot. Only if someone was standing directly over the square of grass could they tell it had been cut. He used a hose coiled near an outside water tap to water the grass around the graves. In a day or two all signs of his work would be gone.

He was far from done. Back inside, he rearmed the security system for most of the house, leaving the sensors off in the entry, the den, and the small half-bath across the hall from it. In the den he locked the door from the inside, closed all the curtains in the room to turn it dark, opened the hutch, and turned on all the monitors. He could see six of the eight cameras at any one time. He chose one that overlooked the front of the house, and one that panned back and forth across the back. The others were interior cameras that monitored the four entries on the ground floor.

Finally, he moved a Morris chair and hassock so he could sit comfortably and still have a clear view of the monitors. He then pulled a floor lamp over to the chair and turned it on. Just before lowering himself into the chair, he placed several things on a small side table next to it: his laptop computer, the diaries and disks, a cell phone he'd borrowed from Pam, and the gun.

"I'm ready for the siege," he said to the walls. "I just wish I had John Wayne to back me up." He was ready now to crawl back into the lives of the sisters to look for a clue he had apparently missed. He took no joy in the task. He had skimmed over the later part of their lives for a reason: He had not wanted Kate Baker to get older. He had wanted her to stay that beautiful creature, the one who had returned from the war, weary, matured, confident in her abilities, but lost because she had lost the man in her life. That was how he wanted to remember her. That was when he had admired her the most.

He did not want to follow her through to old age. He, like everyone else, would have to make his own journey. As a writer, he could leave Kate Baker forever at this moment in time, as he had when he had written about the three sisters. That story was still there, on the disks. He wouldn't add to it. But he would have to move beyond that point to see what he'd missed.

He picked up Elizabeth's diary and began to read. He decided to start with the most tortured soul, the first one to die.

FOURTEEN

PAUL READ THROUGH Elizabeth's diary, pausing only to eat a wrapped sandwich he brought with him and to open a bottle of flavored water. Occasionally he would scan the monitors to see what was happening outside the den, but mostly he read.

He learned little new from a second, more careful reading of the diary. As a child Elizabeth had been caught between the strong-willed, manipulative, controlling Emily and the equally strong-willed, precocious Kate. Too weak on her own to battle the powers of her two sisters, she survived by hiding out in her bedroom with books, or literally hiding where Emily couldn't find her.

Her revenge came in later years when she tried to wrest control of the ranch from her sisters through marriage. Her plan was to marry, and then, using the terms of the will her mother had left behind, to grab her share of the ranch, and more if she could. She might have succeeded, too, except an engagement to Doc Hollingsworth's son that Emily had brought to an end. Then, her last best bet to control the ranch through marriage to Rodney Ryan ended when he was killed.

The relationship with Rodney left her with syphilis. Even Kate, the best-trained doctor in the valley for her time, couldn't help Elizabeth. In 1935, at the age of 49,

Elizabeth died from the disease, her brain eaten away by it. She was little more than a vegetable when she died. Kate had spent the vast majority of three years doing little more than caring for her dying sister.

Most of the few entries in the last five years of Elizabeth's diary were incoherent ramblings. Paul doubted that even a Freudian psychologist could have made much of it. The rest of the entries, before that and after Rodney's death, were tirades against her sisters. She believed that the sisters had conspired to keep her from getting what was rightfully hers. Each of these tirades was followed by long passages filled with self-pity. If nothing else, Elizabeth understood her fate. Her chances had passed her by, and now she was at the mercy of the sisters.

He closed the diary and put it on the table. He needed a break. He walked into the hall to the control panel, and turned off the sensors inside of the house. He then wandered through the lower floor, first into the parlor and then to the kitchen in the back. From there he walked into the dining room with its French doors that opened onto a portico. He had his hand on the doorknob before he remembered that he had not turned off the alarms to the doors.

He pulled his hand away and stared out across the lawn, to the irrigation ditch, and then to the trees beyond. The irrigation ditch used to run down the hillside to the fields below, but it had since been diverted through the trees, eventually going under the surrounding fence of the estate through a culvert. Upstream, just inside the gates, was a pond formed behind a damn that Silas Baker, the sisters' father, had built to store up water for the dry summers. The pond was only a fraction of the size it had been in Silas's day. The original timbers that

made up the face of the dam were still there, and the
iron wheel on top that pulled up a metal plate behind
the timbers to let out water was still in place, too. It was
on the top of this dam that a rattlesnake had bitten Silas
and had killed him.

Paul walked from the dining room back to the den.
He picked up Emily's diary and took it with him as he
climbed the stairs in the entry to the second floor. He
threw open the double doors to the master bedroom. It
was much like it had been, except now the curtains were
thrown open and light flooded the room. He ran his hand
over the cherry wood of the bed. This had been such a
sad place. Yes, Kate had been born in this room, but her
mother had locked herself away in here, with the curtains
shut tightly and the fire in the fireplace blazing hot in
winter and summer. Emily had spent much of the last
years of her life in the same way, curtains closed and
fire burning, enfolded in the cream and white silk lace
of the bedding.

She did it both because she was a true product of her
mother and because she knew how much it infuriated
Kate. At least she'd surrounded herself with a fairly
good library of books and a record player, so she hadn't
just sat up here and sulked.

He sat in a chair next to the fireplace and thumbed
through Emily's diary, refreshing his memories about
her reasons for sulking. Until Kate returned from the
war, Emily had run the ranch. She hadn't been very good
at it, a fact she slowly came to realize as profits disappeared and she began to cut into capital. It hadn't taken
Kate long to right the ship after her return. She made
some key decisions that saved the Baker estate: sold
some of their land for top dollar, purchased much
cheaper grazing land in eastern Oregon, and moved the

livestock there. She used some of the profit to make needed repairs to the ranch and to modernize, which reduced the need for manpower, and then she carefully invested the rest.

Much of Emily's diary after the war years was filled with grudging admiration for the way Kate had saved the estate, had turned the Depression to their advantage, and had accumulated millions of dollars. That wasn't good enough for Emily, though. She saw no purpose in having the money if they didn't have an heir to leave it to. And, of course, there was an heir, Oliver Baker. She never forgave Kate for giving up her child, and many passages in the diary plotted how she would out-live Kate and see that the estate went to Oliver.

She did not out-live Kate. She died in 1955, at the age of 73, a short time before Kate died.

The light was fading when he finished with Emily's diary. He closed the book and let it sit on his lap. He hadn't learned anything enlightening from it. Mostly, in the later years, it was filled with petty grievances. Emily felt that Kate ran her life, and she got even in small ways: refusing to leave her room for weeks on end, refusing to sign the tax forms, refusing to talk to her sister for days. She also gloated about small victories, although Paul couldn't fathom what they were. She wrote about them in a cryptic way, apparently afraid that Kate might read her diary and find out. Only one brief statement caught Paul's attention.

One event, just before her death, seemed to please her the most. Unfortunately, the only reference to it in the diary said, "I got her good this time." Beyond that, whatever it was, he could find nothing in the diary that would explain the current mystery.

He closed up the bedroom and returned to the hall,

once again arming the sensors in all the rooms except those he was using. From the same control panel, he turned on the floodlights that illuminated the yard all around the house. He checked the monitors when he got back to the den. He still had a clear view of the property near the house should anyone try to approach.

He sat in the chair with Kate Baker's diary in his lap. Surprisingly, the diary provided only a minimal amount of information about the sisters and their later lives. He learned about Elizabeth's last years from Emily's diary. He learned about Kate's battles with Emily from Elizabeth's diary. Mostly, in her later years, Kate recorded events. She recorded the death of her uncle, Silas's brother, Tim, who'd raised Oliver as his own son. She noted when Oliver went to college. She had clippings from a local newspaper about Oliver becoming a flying ace during World War II. She had another article that announced when he became an ace during the Korean War.

Paul wondered what she would have thought of that. Both she and Oliver's father had been doctors, desperately trying to save lives during the First World War. They had produced a man whose primary claim to fame was his ability to kill during war. He had shot down twenty-seven planes during World War II. He had been shot down twice, one time to be rescued at sea, and a second time that required him to work his way back to England through enemy-held territory.

In the Korean War, he had eleven kills. He hadn't been shot down. The rules of the game had changed by then. Jets had replaced prop-driven planes. Missiles had replaced cannons. To get shot down meant a big chance of getting killed.

Whatever tricks that Emily had pulled on Kate did not

show up in Kate's diary. Nor did the slow devastation of the Baker estate. Kate had much of her plan in place, waiting for the day when Emily died to carry it out. The security fence had already been built around the grounds. The irrigation ditch had been diverted so she could have the eroding slope in front of the house cut away and a concrete and stone retaining wall put up in its place. She intended for the house to be preserved forever, a monument on the hillside to the frustration of the Bakers' lives.

Shortly before Emily died, Kate began selling off everything she could, giving the gains away to charities. In her will she allocated even more to other causes. What she could not foresee was that she would die shortly after, not quite finished with her plan. The best she could do, after she discovered that she was dying, was to rewrite her will in a way that tied up the assets she had stuffed in safe deposit boxes. She must have done a good job of it, because even Pam couldn't get to the money.

He closed the diary, no wiser than he had been. He fell asleep feeling sorry for Kate Baker, a woman who deserved so much more from life than she got, but also a woman who may well have been her own worst enemy.

Paul didn't know what woke him. It might have been a noise, or it might have been the flickering pattern of light in front of him. All six of the monitors showed electronic snow. Something had caused the pictures to go out. He got up from the chair and moved to the windows. He pulled one curtain back just a fraction to look outside. What he saw was complete darkness. The floodlights were out.

The man in black was here.

He glanced around the room. Everything he had

worked so hard to protect was here for the taking. He gathered up the three diaries and scanned the den for a place to hide them. He couldn't bear to give the diaries up. To himself he said, "If it worked for Poe, maybe it'll work for me," thinking of Edgar Allen Poe's short story, "The Purloined Letter." The letter had been "hidden" by leaving it out in plain sight.

He pulled three books from one of the bookshelves which lined the walls on each side of the fireplace, and replaced them with the diaries. He then pulled the chair and side table back to where they had been and placed the three books on the table, as if they were on display.

The packet of disks was something else again. If the man got in, he certainly would take the computer and the disks with him if he could. Again Paul scanned the room. He didn't have much time, he was sure. If the guy could cut the signal to the monitors and killed the floodlights, the doors wouldn't stop him. He looked at the bookshelves again. He might be able to put a disk inside a number of books, but he wasn't sure he had the time for that.

And then he got an idea. The fireplace. He walked over, pulled the screen away, and reached an arm up inside. He found the flue, a metal plate hinged to open and close. The lever to control it was inside the fireplace, near the front. He pulled it down. The flue dropped open. He reached through the opening. The chimney was bigger than the flue opening. He could feel a ledge up inside. He reached up with the disks and set them on the ledge, closing the flue plate when he was done.

That took care of the disks and the diaries. The computer wouldn't be as easy to hide. Again he searched the room. He nearly tripped over the answer, literally. The toe of his shoe caught on the floor grate in front of the

windows. Pam had put in forced-air heating to help preserve the house. He pulled off the grate and looked inside. The ductwork was made of metal. The opening
dropped down about eighteen inches and then took a
right turn. He lowered the computer down in the hole
until it was completely out of sight, and then he put the
grate back on.

He then grabbed the gun and cell phone and headed
out the door. He scrambled as fast as he could upstairs.
He had just made it to the first landing when all the lights
in the house went out, including the little flashing red
ones below the panel box that said the system was armed
and operating.

He didn't stop climbing until he reached the attic
rooms, the ones in which the help had lived when the
sisters were alive. He knew how to get out of one of
those windows and make his way down to the ground.
He had done it before, when he'd added ''cat burglar''
to his résumé while researching the sisters' lives.

He found the window, turned the latch, and lifted.
Nothing happened. He pushed a little harder. The window didn't budge. He ran his hand around the seam
between the window and frame to see if it had been
freshly painted. It wasn't paint that he found—he found
screws instead. Apparently, so the security company
wouldn't have to put a sensor on every window in the
house, they'd screwed some of them closed from the
inside. Since this was not a part of the house that anyone
would see, Paul guessed that all the windows in the attic
got the same treatment. If the man was in the house
below, Paul was trapped up here.

Cell phones were made for emergencies, he told himself, and this was an emergency. He dialed 911. When
a voice answered, he said, "I'm Paul Fischer and I'm

staying at the Baker house. Someone is outside, trying to break in.''

A female voice, calm and reassuring, said the wrong words. ''I'm sorry, Mr. Fischer, but security for the Baker house is handled by Master Protection. We refer all calls to them.''

''This is an emergency. I think the guy's got a gun.''

''We suggest you call Master Protection and share that information with them. We do not have access to the estate, and they do. If they believe the situation to be serious, they'll call us.''

''I don't have the number.''

''It should be posted on the alarm panels and next to the phones in the Baker house.''

He tried to sound desperate, but the situation was too comic. ''I'm in the attic, talking to you on a cell phone. I don't dare go back down to look up a phone number.''

She paused. ''I will call Master Protection and notify the police,'' she finally said.

She terminated the call. Suddenly he felt a bit foolish. Maybe all of this was caused by some kind of short. If the terminals shorted out, they might have triggered a series of failures, including first the floodlights and then all the power.

That thought reassured him for about two seconds. The alarm system would have had a backup power source, and it too was out.

He moved to the darkest corner of the room and sat on the floor with his back against a wall. He had the gun and a clear view of the door. That was the only advantage he had.

DOWNSTAIRS, THE MAN slipped the locks on the French doors into the dining room and let himself in. For him, a lock was about the same as a doorknob for getting into a room. The rest of the security system had been more of a challenge, for about five minutes. He had quickly sorted through the wires at the power box on the outside of the house. A shunt between two wires shorted out the video receiver in the house. Two more shunts shorted out the power while frying the backup power for the alarm system.

As he quietly let himself into the house, he made a mental note. He thought someday he'd have his own security service, so he kept track of the things that might have made his entry unsuccessful. They should have moved the power box to the inside of the basement and buried the incoming line underground. He would have still been able to get in, eventually, but he wouldn't have risked the kind of time it would have taken.

He knew where Fischer had been, and he was sure he wasn't there anymore. He eased open the door to the den and poked the silenced gun into the room. He paused to listen. Years ago he had developed the skill to listen completely, one of the reasons he was so good at what he did. He could block out all sounds but those coming from the room. Nothing. Fischer was gone from the room.

He had followed Fischer's movement around the house from the safety of the woods. When the light was good, he could see through the windows and watch Paul move around the house. When the sun went down, he followed him by the lights that went on and off. Even though Paul had closed the curtains to the den, enough light filtered through to know that was where he was.

Or had been. He had already learned that Fischer was clever enough, although no match for himself. He knew that Fischer would go into hiding as soon as the lights went out. He also knew that he would try to sound an alarm, so he cut the phone lines. In the good old days, that was enough, but this was the age of wireless communication. He set a mental clock to ticking in the back of his head. He had ten minutes. No more. If Fischer had a cell phone, that was how long it would take for the security guards to arrive on the scene. Then he had another ten minutes. Once the guards saw that the security system had been breached, they would call the local police and wait for them to arrive before they did anything.

That was more than enough time to get what he wanted from Fischer, and then to kill him.

UPSTAIRS, PAUL WAS practicing the art of listening, too. He'd spent enough time in the house, including the weekend two years ago, that he knew its sounds. Like most old houses, it creaked and cracked its way through changes in temperatures and moisture. It would have a new sound, too, of the forced-air heating, but the temperature was mild so it wasn't on. Anything beyond those sounds would be the intruder. The first sound the man made came from the den. Paul recognized it immediately. He was lifting the grate from the floor.

THE MAN SMILED to himself. Finding the computer had been a cinch. The disks had taken only a few minutes more. Again he had listened, and this time he had heard the slight sound of air escaping up the chimney from the flue not quite closed. That sound had not been there the last time he had been in this room.

The diaries took a little longer. He hadn't known what he was looking for, only that three books were on the end table now that hadn't been there before, and he could spot no obvious place on the bookshelves where those three books had been.

The diaries stood out because they were shorter than the books on the either side of them. He only had to read the first page of one of them to know this was what he had been searching for, the thing that would give him the clue he needed. He piled his find on the seat of the chair, and then he quickly went through the room to see if he had missed anything.

He would have just enough time to get back and grab these things after he killed Fischer and before the police came. He left the den and walked out to the landing. Fischer would have gone upstairs. To run outside would be to run into the unknown. He would be hiding somewhere up there, probably in the attic. The man had little time to fool around looking for him.

He shouted up the stairs, "Fischer, I'm coming up there and I'm going to kill you." He listened. Yes, he could hear the shuffling in the attic room near the front of the house.

PAUL SCRAMBLED TO his feet when he heard the voice. Logic told him to sit still and be quiet, but the words alone pushed his flight button. He had the moonlight coming through the window, but that wasn't enough to give him an advantage. If anything, it would allow the intruder to see where he *wasn't* in the room. Paul pulled a chair away from a tiny desk in the room, and took it to the door, wedging it under the doorknob. That would hold the door for about two good jolts.

He could hear the footsteps coming up the stairs. The man was making no attempt to be quiet. He was either foolish or absolutely fearless. Paul guessed fearless, and that scared him even more. Paul would have to think hard first before he could fire the gun at the man. The man wouldn't think at all, he'd simply kill him.

That was all the reasoning he needed. He quickly tossed the mattress from the single bed in the room and pulled out one of the wood slats that supported it. Using it as a ram, he methodically began to knock out the window glass and frame.

THE MAN HEARD the noise and knew what it was. If he got there quickly enough, he could shoot Fischer before he made it out the window, or he could shoot him on the roof. He ran up the stairs, reaching the door in nearly full stride and hit it full force. He expected it to crack open and catch Fischer completely by surprise. Instead it held for just a fraction of a second, and then he found himself crashing head over heals through a pile of wood debris. He never paused for a moment, rolling over the obstruction and springing to his feet with his gun pointed toward the window. Too late. Fischer was already outside.

He whirled around and ran down the stairs as quickly as he had come up them. He didn't pause in the entry, but ran down the hallway, into the dining room and through the French doors. He could hear Fischer dropping to the ground from the front porch roof.

PAUL CRUMPLED to the ground after he dropped from the roof, and struggled to push himself to his feet, panic eating away at him. He had to get away. The only thing that came to mind that would put the kind of distance between them that he needed was to go down the bluff. He sprinted across the lawn and placed one hand around one of the spearheads on the iron fence before vaulting over it.

In that tiny instant of time his brain registered its first bit of logic in his flood of panic: It remembered that the drop was forty feet, nearly straight down. Although his body willed itself away from danger, his brain got the message out just in time for his hand not to let go. Paul found himself swinging around and slamming into the outside of the fence. There he dangled over the long drop by a hand that wasn't about to release its grip.

From here he had a good view of the intruder coming around the corner of the house. The man stopped. He lifted his arm and pointed it at Paul. There was no doubt in Paul's mind what was on the end of the arm. He let his hand go and dropped...four feet, until it hooked on the bottom rail of the fence. He heard the *ppfff* of the silenced gunshot.

Paul looked down into the darkness below him. He was stunned to see the gun in his right hand. In his panic, he had forgotten he had it. Without thought, he lifted the gun over his head and aimed it in the direction of the intruder, firing three quick shots.

The man instinctively dove to the ground at the sight of the first flash from the gun. He rolled toward the house, into the shadows along the foundation. As quick as a cat, he was on his hands and knees, backing away from the fence. When he was sure it was safe to stand, he took off running around the house. He came around the other side and moved to the front of the yard, squeezing himself between the graves and the fence. He knew that Fischer was hanging by his left arm and firing with his right. That meant his back would be to him if he came up to Fischer along the fence.

The plan was a good one. It was only missing one element: Fischer. He was no longer hanging from the fence when the man sneaked a peek over the edge. He had to have fallen. Hopefully the fall had killed him. The man no longer had time to worry about him. He could see the main highway from where he stood, could see the three police cars racing up the hill with their lights blazing. He ran back to the house and rounded the corner. In the distance, back by the main gate, he could see more flashing lights. He desperately needed to get back in the house to get the diaries, but now he wasn't sure if he could risk it. The shots fired might bring the security guards in before the cops arrived. He dashed across the yard to the trees. When he reached the fence, he followed it to the irrigation ditch. In the water, he rolled over on his back and floated down to the culvert. There was just enough room above water for his nose when the water swept him through the underground concrete pipe.

PAUL WAS NOT stretched out on the ground below. As soon as he had fired and then heard the intruder retreating, he had stuffed the gun in his back pocket and then worked his way, handhold by handhold, along the length of the bluff until he'd moved into the deep shadows away from the house.

He had listened to the man return, and then he had heard him make a hasty retreat through the woods. Paul didn't waste a minute. He pulled back up, feeling like he was going to rip his arms from their sockets every inch of the way, and finally deposited himself back in the yard. He ran quickly to the house, and around to the side from where the intruder had come and found the open French doors.

He was relieved to see the neat stack on the chair and a little surprised. He thought he had hidden all the items well. Obviously the man was clever. He grabbed the diaries, the disks and his knapsack. A few moments later he was back at the grave site rolling back the patch of grass. He dug frantically until he reached the box. Fortunately the dirt was still loose and the digging went fast. Although it seemed like forever to him, he had the diaries back in place within two or three minutes. He put the gun and disks in the knapsack and tossed them together over the fence, far enough so they would clear the road below and land in the thick bushes on the other side. He hoped he got back to them before some kid found them.

He was just walking around the corner of the house when several lights blinded him and a booming voice ordered him to drop to the ground with his arms spread out in front of him.

FIFTEEN

PAUL HAD A LONG VISIT with the security people and the police. The security company knew from Pam that he was staying in the house. What they wanted to know was the sequence of the outages so they could not only repair the damage, but also prevent the same thing from happening in the future.

Paul wasn't much help to them. He'd had his own agenda to take care of when the man was getting into the house. He could have been more help to the police, but chose not to be: He didn't want to explain the gun to them. He wasn't sure what the laws were in Oregon for the possession of a weapon, and he didn't want to find out what they were by being charged with violating one of them.

He walked the police through the sequence of events, leading them up to the attic to show them the broken window and door. He explained to them how he had climbed down from the third floor to the roof of the porch, and how he had been forced to jump because he could hear the intruder coming out of the house.

Explaining the gun shots was easy. He told the police that the intruder had fired at him, which was true. Of course the man had only fired one shot, not three, but he would let him explain that to the police, should he ever get the chance.

The cops were pretty skeptical when he told them about dangling from the fence and then working his way down to the shadows. He earned a little more respect from them when he borrowed a flashlight and shined it on the slope below, showing them where the toes of his shoes had scuffed the surface of the wall.

Finally he talked one of them into driving him back to Pam's. He was in no mood to play more night-stalker games with the intruder, so he had the cop wait while he got his things out of the guest cottage and loaded them into the Alfa. The cop followed him out of the driveway, turning right toward Medford after Paul turned left.

The sun was just coming up, and Paul wanted to find the gun before someone else did. As he drove back toward the Baker house, he pondered the one question he could not answer for the police: Why had the man tried to kill him? He hadn't bothered to tell the cops about the incident in the orchard, which would only confuse them. It certainly confused Paul. The man could have killed him then. Why not then and why now?

As he pulled onto the access road, the answer was obvious: When the guy came out of the house to try to kill Paul, he thought he had the diaries and disks; he didn't need Paul anymore. Paul thought about that: If there was something in that information he wanted to know, why get rid of Paul? Didn't he know more about the sisters than anyone?

The answer to that came to him slowly, if not very clearly. The guy needed the diaries to find something he knew about, but it must be something that Paul didn't know about. But what? Paul had been rough that material in-depth now. He had read all three diaries through.

He could find nothing in any of them that gave him a clue to all of this. What had he missed?

He walked into the brush and tall grass across the road. It took him about five minutes, but he finally found the knapsack with the gun still inside. He returned to the car and folded down the convertible top. He tossed the knapsack on the floor and got inside to start the car. As he pulled away, he decided he needed to do two things: First, find out when Pam's plane would be coming in; he wanted to be at the airport to meet her. Second, he needed to buy some more bullets for the gun. From now on, he and the gun would not be too far apart.

In the meantime, he needed a place to stay. He had no second thoughts about that. He drove the car back to the main highway and worked his way toward Jacksonville, the former gold town that had been such a significant part of the Bakers' lives. He didn't stop. He continued out of town on Old Stage Coach Road and kept going until he had threaded his way through the back country to emerge finally in Ashland. There he decided to splurge a little of his savings and stay in the Mark Antony Hotel, right in the middle of town and only a few blocks from the Shakespearean Festival's three theaters. Paul wasn't going to be caught alone in the dark by this guy again.

He was lucky to get a room. The Shakespearean Festival brought visitors from around the world for nearly nine months of the years. Tickets to plays and hotel rooms were always at a premium, but because people had to book so far in advance, it was not unusual to see a cancellation because of something they could not have foreseen when they made their reservations.

He had a corner room six floors up with a good view of Ashland and the valley stretching out toward Medford. He made it clear at the desk that under no circumstances were they to confirm to anyone that he was registered here. He considered other options when he got to his room: A few days of not shaving, sunglasses, and a hat would do wonders to hide his identity. The Alfa would have to go back; he'd get something less obvious and go underground.

And then he wondered why he should bother with all that. He'd need to keep in touch with Pam. The guy could track him through her. The man had already proven himself to be smarter than anything in his way. What would stop him from finding Paul again? Paul decided: Not much. The best thing then was to make sure that the man never caught Paul alone. The next confrontation would have to be in front of a crowd of people. Satisfied with that answer, Paul began to unpack his things. He pulled out the Baker disks from inside his computer carrying case; perhaps in here was a clue he had missed.

He turned on the computer and popped in the first disk. He began to read again about Oliver Baker.

HE WAS AT the airport when Pam's plane arrived at 5:30 that afternoon. She was surprised to find him there, but she handled it gracefully, introducing him to each of her fellow travelers. He shook hands, smiled, and shared greetings. Although no one asked, he generously explained to anyone who'd listen that he'd come to pick up Pam. Eventually, even she got the idea that he was there for her.

After the others left to get their bags, she grabbed him by the arm and guided him to the seats in the waiting area, actually shoving him into one of them. "What's up?"

"Have I got that look written all over my face?"

"You look like you haven't slept in a month and like you've lost ten pounds, and I just saw you yesterday."

"Has it only been since yesterday?"

She sank slowly into a chair next to him. "You burned down the house, didn't you?"

"Which house?"

She did a slow take, but even the smile on his face didn't ease her fears. "Any of them."

"The last time I looked, your houses were okay. The Baker house will need a little work, though."

She slumped just a little in her chair. "What kind of work?"

"Promise me you will just sit there and listen. I'll explain everything, but there's a lot to explain. To begin with, the house will need only minor repairs, but the security system may take a little work."

She kept her word. She didn't interrupt him until he was finished, and even then she didn't say anything. That worried him. "I told your security service to keep the estate guarded around the clock until they made the repairs to the system. I also got the number for the caretakers of the estate from the security people and asked them to board up the window and arrange for a carpenter to come in. I hope that was all right."

She nodded slowly. "That's fine. What I want to do is to back up to what you called 'the fun and games' in the orchard. I want to know why you didn't tell me about it in the first place."

That was fair, he thought, except he knew what she was getting at. Instead of ducking it, he approached the subject head on. "I could have shown you the footprints and the broken branches, but I wasn't sure what your reaction would be. You might have thought I was making it up—''

''Which is unlikely,'' she said, interrupting.

''Which was unlikely.''

''So there had to be another reason.''

''Yeah,'' he said, ''at least one more. I didn't want you to worry. You had enough on your mind with Chuck's death.''

''And another reason?''

''I thought maybe you might have already known.''

She smiled to herself. ''I was thinking about that on the flight back. I was wondering how much you trusted me now. Beyond a few events that may or may not be related, not much has changed since the last time we were together. I still want the money from the estate. I think it rightfully belongs to me. You still feel the need to protect Kate Baker's will. Let me assure you, though, I'm being up-front with you.''

''And I'll be up-front with you. The guy tried to kill me this time. I don't doubt he killed Chuck. I don't doubt that he'll try to kill you and maybe Nora. I think he's after something, and he's afraid that if he leaves us alive, we'll get to it first, or we'll find a way to keep him from having it.''

''But what is there beside the money in the estate? He couldn't get it if he wanted. I mean if I couldn't get it out, how could he?''

''I don't know,'' Paul said. ''It's something we don't know about; we've got to find out what that is.''

She stood up slowly, looking very tired. ''Let's go back to my house and talk about it.''

He got up, too. ''Sorry,'' he said, ''but I'm not going back.'' He told her where he was staying. ''I don't recommend you go back, especially at night and without an armed guard. I'm sure one of those people on the plane can put you up."

"How many beds in your room?" she asked.

The surprise showed on his face when he looked at her. "Two."

"A good number," she said. "I'll get my suitcase. I still have some clean clothes in it. We'll both have a better chance of thinking this through if we can get some sleep and you're the only one I trust right now."

She walked off toward the baggage area, forcing him to hustle to catch up to her. As he fell in stride with her, he asked, "Does this mean we're going steady?"

"You don't even get kissed, on the first date, buster, so don't even start dreaming dreams of conquest."

"That's fine," he said. "I'll take any kind of dreams. Last night I only had nightmares."

SIXTEEN

HE WOKE UP the next morning and stared at Pam Livingston's curled-up figure in the bed next to his. He couldn't see her face. She slept with her back to him, her hair spread across the side of her face.

The blanket on the bed conformed to the shape of her body, outlining the sleek curve of her from thigh to shoulder. He admired it. He sat up in bed, trying to remember what it was like to make love to her. Little came back. It had been a time of deception, and the lovemaking had been lost in the intrigue. He remembered her to be beautiful, her body breathtaking, and her lovemaking satisfying. But he couldn't remember the details.

She stirred under his stare and mumbled, ''Are you ogling me?''

He thought about a lot of things he could have said to deny it, but instead he said, ''How'd you know?''

''I had this vague feeling once before that you admired me for my body. I just wanted to make sure I hadn't lost any of my appeal.''

''So if I'd said no, you'd have been disappointed?''

''I probably would've joined a health club and worked out every day for a month.''

''Wow. I didn't know I had that kind of power.''

''You don't. It just shows you how insecure I've become in my old age.''

"You're in your early thirties. That's not exactly old age."

"It's all downhill from here." She rolled over so she could see him. "You've picked up a few gray hairs yourself, you know."

"Yeah, but I'm not self-conscious about it."

"That's what I hate about men."

"Don't tell me you're giving up on us."

"That's the only thing I hate about men. Now be a gentleman and turn your back while I slip into the bathroom."

He did as he was told, waiting until he heard her weight lift off the bed before stealing a glimpse. What he saw made him smile. She wore a T-shirt to bed which didn't quite hang down low enough to cover her bare bottom. The sight helped him remember a lot more about her that had slipped his mind. She spent a long time in the bathroom, and when she emerged she was wearing a bathrobe supplied by the hotel and had a matching white towel wrapped around her head. "I'm going to do the unheard of," she said. "I'm going to call in to work and tell them I'm taking the day off."

"A day off. Is that unusual?"

She laughed. "Actually, I'm not taking the day off. I've got my computer with me, and I have lots of work to do. I just don't need to go into the office. I usually have one day a week when I don't schedule appointments with clients so I can keep up with the paperwork." She sat on the bed with her legs curled up under her, looking relaxed.

He didn't want to break the spell. "Why don't you order breakfast to be brought up while I take my shower? I do have some things I want to go over with you."

"Like what?"

''I'd like to continue our conversation from when I got here: I'd like to know more about what you think about your father. You seem to have some issues with him.''

''My father is a nice man.'' She said it far too quickly, as if it was something that had been practiced.

''I'm talking about Oliver Baker.''

''I don't think of him as being my father,'' she said. ''He died before I was born.''

''What do you know about him?''

''I know he was more concerned about his career than he was about his family. I know he volunteered once too often to go off to war. I know he tested fate one too many times and it killed him. I know all of that.''

To Paul it sounded like Pam's view of her father might well have been a mother's view projected on the daughter, angry at being widowed. ''That doesn't answer my question.'' He bent over the side of the bed and removed some papers from his briefcase. He tossed them across the gap between them to Pam. ''These are chapters of a book written about your father. A man wrote them who had served with your father. It's one of those books you only find on the bookshelf in a library on a military base. But if anything, I think it captures the essence of your father. Now, order breakfast, read these chapters, and don't look while I get out of bed.''

If he expected her to look, he was only moderately disappointed. She was too busy reading through the pages he gave her to notice him.

The story she read was about the event that led to the last days of Colonel Oliver Baker. A flying Ace from two wars, he was reduced to flying recon missions in Vietnam to test new equipment. He took the job gladly. The alternative was to be sent back to the States to do flight training. He was thought too old to fly in combat, a decision that he could barely tolerate.

He and his co-pilot, Lieutenant Jay McIntire, were flying at night—in a Mohawk, a highly maneuverable twin-prop plane used for reconnaissance—over a valley suspected of being a base for the Vietcong. The plane was packed full of the latest sensing equipment to locate the enemy.

The equipment was good, but the pilots were still learning to use it. It was too late when Baker and McIntire confirmed the valley was indeed full of the enemy. Heavy fire from below sent their plane plowing into the jungle.

Both McIntire and Baker survived, but McIntire was severely injured. Baker was injured too, but not so extensively that he couldn't pull them both from the burning plane and drag McIntire to safety. An intensive search for them by the Vietcong was interrupted by an air attack from friendly sources. The valley was extensively bombed to make sure that none of the equipment on the plane came into enemy hands.

Both McIntire and Baker were nearly killed in the bombing. Again Baker managed to save them both and start them on a three-day journey toward friendly territory. He had to carry McIntire most of the way. The enemy tracked them throughout the entire three days. In the book, McIntire described the hair-raising hour when Baker called for a rescue team, the transmission allowing the Viet Cong to locate them. Baker held the enemy at bay while a helicopter came in to rescue McIntire. When a rescue squad moved in to save Baker, it was already too late; he had been captured. Rumor had it he was tortured and then executed. His remains were turned over to the U.S. government after the war, and, true to his wife's wishes, his ashes were scattered over the Gulf of Tonkin.

When he got out of the shower and rejoined Pam in the room, breakfast still hadn't been ordered. Instead, Pam sat with the pages of paper in her lap and stared out a window into the distance.

SEVENTEEN

HE ORDERED BREAKFAST. When it came, they ate it in silence. He desperately wanted to know what she was thinking, but he also knew he couldn't push Pam into doing something she didn't want to do.

When they'd finished eating and were sitting back with their cups of coffee, she finally asked, "Why did you want me to read that?"

"I think most of us would be curious to know what other people thought of our parents, especially if it was positive. This is the Oliver Baker I know. I'm wondering if I know more about him than you do."

"Probably," she said sarcastically. "I know Oliver was my father and he was probably Kate's son, making her my grandmother."

"Knowing Kate is your grandmother and proving it are two different things. What I want to know is what you think of Oliver Baker."

"He was a comic-book hero."

"Lieutenant McIntire didn't think so. He's the one who wrote the book, and in it you can see why. He admired and respected your father long before that incident, and then he grew to love the colonel when he first saved the lieutenant's life, and then sacrificed his own so that the lieutenant could be rescued. He thought that might get her curious, but he was disappointed by her response.

"What's this got to do with anything? The colonel, as the socially correct in this valley still call him, died a long time ago. So he was a man's man, but that doesn't change the kind of husband he was, or the fact that he didn't stay around to be a father."

"The staying around to be a father was a choice he might have made, but given the circumstances he would have had to choose between his life and the lieutenant's. At the time fatherhood hadn't come into it; I don't even know if he knew your mother was pregnant with you. If you are angry because he didn't stick around to be your father, I'm not sure you have a good reason for it. No, what came into play was the simple fact that Oliver Baker believed he could defy the odds one more time. No one knows for sure what he thought when he found out he couldn't. Let's look at it another way. I reread the diaries. I couldn't find anything in them that would explain what's going on here. I didn't have time to review my research material, but I'm pretty sure the information isn't in it, either. That means we have to look someplace else. I thought we'd start with your father."

He didn't add that he had read something in Emily's diary that related to Oliver, something that indeed might explain what the intruder was looking for.

She was leaning against the headboard of her bed, the coffee cup in her lap and was staring at him with an expression that was more a lawyer than a friend. "You hid the diaries at the house," she said. "You must have done a damned good job of it, considering the amount of looking we did."

"I hid the diaries at the house, but that doesn't mean they're still there."

"Right. And where else might they be?"

"Maybe they're buried in the orchard next to your house. Maybe they're in this room."

She laughed. "They're not in this room."

"And how do you know that?"

"I looked through your things while you were in the shower."

"Are we back to being adversaries?"

"Right, and you didn't peek when I got out of bed."

He smiled. "I'd have to have suppressed all of my maleness to not look."

"And I would have had to hide all my Baker pride to not look for the diaries."

"But the pride doesn't extend to your father."

That stopped her. No witty replies this time. The lawyer look came back to her face. "It's pretty hard," she said, "to love someone who is only a legend. On one hand I've been fed press clippings and faded photos; on the other hand I've listened to my mother tell me how she had begged him not to go back to Vietnam."

"You know why he went."

"He was trying to salvage a career that had run its course."

"He always believed he could get back to the glory days. Silas Baker had his land. Emily had her power. Kate had her fortune. Oliver had his fame. None of them handled what they had in the best way they could, perhaps, but they all had much more than most people get and they did what they could with it, good or bad. It must have been hard to be a legend and a hero, and to have to go out with a slow fade instead of a burst of glory."

"I'm supposed to feel sympathy?"

"I don't know. I have the rest of the book. I downloaded it from the Internet. Read it and decide for yourself.''

''I won't get any work done.''

''Yeah, that's probably right.''

She reached out a hand. ''I once had a counselor tell me I needed to come to terms with my real father. Let me warn you, though, I still want to hate him.''

He removed the rest of the manuscript from his briefcase next to the bed. The book had been used by all four services at their military academies as a text on escape and jungle survival. McIntire had been a good writer. He got all the details in. He made the work even more appealing by writing from the colonel's point of view. Since he was the last person to spend any significant time with the colonel, no one doubted this view. Paul handed her the rest of the book.

EIGHTEEN

HE HADN'T BEEN HAPPY since he'd had to flee from the Baker House, and now he was even less happy. The two of them, the lawyer and the college prof, had given him the slip. Nobody gave him the slip.

He still had the gnawing feeling in the pit of his stomach that he'd been had by a wimp, an Ivy League college teacher. He knew part of it had been pure luck on Fischer's part to get away, but the fact that he had let pure luck play any part in it added to his anger. He never figured the professor would have a gun.

He'd spent two days trying to undo the damage. Everything had gone wrong. When he went back to the Baker house, he found the place crawling with security and repair people. He hadn't been able to get too close, but what he could see from the woods wasn't too reassuring. It looked like they were making the kinds of changes to the security system he would have made himself. He was pretty sure he could still get inside, but it would take a lot more effort now than before.

He doubted that Fischer had left the diaries in the house, but he wanted to get inside to find out for sure. He'd already gone through both Livingston's house and guesthouse when he figured out they weren't coming back. He hadn't found a thing he hadn't found before.

Lawyers just couldn't walk away from their practices,

so he was sure he could locate Livingston through her office, and that would lead him to Fischer, except his phone calls had only made the secretary suspicious.

He tried Nora Ryan next, slipping into her office when her back was turned and scaring the crap out of her when she turned to find herself locked inside with him.

The only thing to come of that was the satisfaction of knowing that he had Ryan's attention. She'd been doing some research, but what she gave him wasn't anything he didn't already know. To make matters worse, neither Livingston nor Fischer had been in touch with her. She was definitely on the outside of the information loop, and now he felt she was expendable.

He really wanted Fischer to be expendable, too, but he needed him to get to the diaries. He slumped down in the seat of his car and threw his head back against the headrest. He was parked a block and a half down the street from the lawyer's office building. From where he sat, he could just make out her parking spot. He'd know when she came back. He couldn't miss that big, bright yellow Mercedes. When this was all over, he might just get himself one, too.

He sat perfectly still in the car, his eyes half closed and out of focus. He had learned to sit like this for hours, able to slip into a mindless state while he waited. He'd done it often enough, waiting for one enemy or another. It would only take a flash of yellow to snap him alert.

AT THE SAME TIME the man was waiting for Pam to return to her office, she was back at her house with Paul, where they met two sheriff's deputies. Although the intruder had been good, he'd had to go through too many things in too short a time; both Paul and Pam were able to show the deputies several indications that the man had broken into both houses.

Paul packed up all his things, dressed in his suit, and then put his belongings in the trunk of Pam's Mercedes. Pam, too, packed suitcases. She made arrangements with her cleaning lady to watch the house, and with the maintenance service she used to take care of the grounds. When she had everything together, she and Paul said goodbye to each other.

He headed back to Ashland for his interview. She drove to the Baker house to meet with her secretary and the security people. By evening she and Paul would be living at the Baker house.

ON A WHIM, Paul decided to take the back roads to Jacksonville before driving up to the Baker house. He knew he was taking a risk, still driving the Alfa, but it was another gorgeous day and he couldn't resist putting the top down.

He pulled up beside the museum in Jacksonville and parked. He decided to stop in and see Nora Ryan. He found her, in a fashion, locked in her office, talking through a bolted door before she grudgingly unlocked it and let him in. As soon as he entered the office, she bolted the door again.

"I can understand your caution," he said, looking for a place to sit, "but isn't this a bit much?" If anything, the office was stacked with more odds and ends than he remembered, so many boxes, bundles of papers, and assorted bric-a-brac that he couldn't find a place to sit. He couldn't even find a place to lean. He was left to stand awkwardly in front of Nora as she returned to the only chair in the room.

Without apology she said, "Damned stuff piled up

while I was gone. More cleaned-out attics full of antique crap. Most of it should have been thrown out with the trash, but somebody let out the word that if you donate it to a museum you can get a tax write-off. A tax write-off for garbage."

He looked around the room. He saw a number of flintlock guns leaning here and there, at least three old pitchers with matching bowls, and several kerosene lamps with painted shades. If only a part of the items in unopened boxes and bags were half as valuable, he wouldn't classify any of it as garbage. "If you don't need it," he said, "why don't you sell it in your gift shop and use the proceeds to help support the museum?"

"Because the first time I start doing that," she snapped back, "the yahoos who gave it to me will think to sell it themselves. The cash they'd get would far exceed the money they would save on their taxes. And then we'd stop getting that one little gem in a thousand that gets dumped in my office on a regular basis. What the hell are you doing here?"

"I just came by to see how you're doing. I heard you went back to work. The last time we talked, it didn't look like you'd be doing that."

She waved a hand in the air and said, "The nice thing about being old is you don't have to explain anything you do to anyone."

The subject had just been dismissed, he decided. He glanced around again and tried to be casual as he asked, "Have you been doing any research into the Bakers?"

One eyebrow on the owlish face shot up. "Why would I do that? I told you I was done with the Bakers."

He admired her face, still with that youthful hint of beauty but he also saw the strain. He thought she'd come back to work because she was strong enough, but she didn't look very strong. If anything, he thought she still looked a bit scared.

"Good. If you're really done with the Bakers, then you won't mind telling me what you know about Katie's gold."

She raised her head very slowly, and then turned to look at him. In the gesture and in the expression on her face was a clear admission that the subject was not new to her. "What do you know about Katie's gold?"

"I don't. I saw something in Emily's diary that referred to Katie's gold."

"You need to talk to Pam Livingston about the Baker finances. I don't know a thing about whether or not Katie had any gold, accounted for or not. In fact, I think the whole subject may well be something you don't want to get into."

"Are you trying to tell me something, Nora?"

"I'm trying to tell you that maybe you've never been in so much danger before in your life."

He almost smiled, but suppressed the notion. She hadn't been around when Chuck Owings had roughed him up and pointed a gun at him. She wouldn't know about the shot fired at him in the orchard, or another sent his way at the Baker house. Yes, she had been assaulted, but that was all behind her now. What would she know about danger?

And then he looked at her, thin and frail, the toughness she displayed a poor imitation of the Nora Ryan he had first met. She certainly knew fear. Maybe she knew more about danger than he gave her credit for.

"Has the man who assaulted you been back?" he asked.

She sat still, looking stoic. At first he thought she wasn't going to say anything, but finally she seemed almost to shrink in the chair and whatever shadow of her old self that remained suddenly faded. She was like a leaf that dropped from the tree and withered before it hit the ground, right before his eyes.

"He's been to my house," she said. "He was waiting for me in here yesterday. I think he's pretty much gotten out of me what he can, and now I'm afraid the next time I see him he'll kill me."

"What did he want?"

"From what he has said to me, I think he's looking for money. I don't know what else he'd want."

He nodded his head, wondering if a rumor of gold was behind this. What he didn't know was whether or not a rumor of gold was true. "Is there any missing gold?"

She shrugged her shoulders. "I don't know. I never found any information that suggested hidden gold. Pam may have, but I'm sure she wouldn't have told me."

"It's kind of funny," he said. "I became fascinated with the Baker women because I couldn't understand why three such beautiful females never married. Yours and Pam's interest in the sisters was to try to prove that one or both of you had a legitimate claim to the millions still left in the estate. Now some complete stranger may have taken an interest because he thinks there might be some hidden gold to find and steal. It would be laughable that these women could generate so much turmoil years after they died, except this guy may be a psychopath. It would be fitting if the rumor proved false and there wasn't any gold."

Nora Ryan didn't share his feelings. She had more pressing concerns. She said, "I can't just sit around and wait for him to come and get me."

"I agree with you," he said. "I suggest you let the

folks who ran the museum while you were gone know that you need more time off. And then I think you need to get some things together and get in your car and drive north, at least to Roseburg or Eugene. Don't go to Grant's Pass—that could be where the guy is staying.''

"I can't just run away," she said. "I have a job; I have a house.''

"You were ready to quit the job just a few days ago. Do you have pets or something at the house that need to be taken care of?''

"Pets? Pets and plants are forms of leeches. I wouldn't own something unless it could take care of itself.''

"Then you could get the cop across the street to watch the house while you're away.''

"I'm not made of money. I can't afford to stay away long.''

He walked over to the door that led to the records room and stopped to look inside. "You make your arrangements. I want to go through whatever might be left in here about the Bakers. If we have any luck at all, we might figure out who this guy is and have him arrested.''

"He's seen and read everything he could about the sisters," she said. "If he didn't find something, I doubt if you will.''

He stepped into the room, saying as he disappeared from her view, "I'm not talking about the sisters," he said. "I'm more interested in Oliver.''

She came to stand in the doorway. "Oliver? The Colonel never grew up. He was determined to play army all his life, and his life came up short because playing army killed him.''

Paul sat down at Nora's computer and turned it on. "I'm pretty sure he knew that Kate was his mother, and

I'm pretty sure he carried within him a deep sense of rejection. Maybe playing army, the one thing he was good at, was his way of escaping from his feelings.''

"You damned writers all think you're psychologists. Why do you give Oliver Baker so much credit?''

"Because," he said, now quickly moving through directories on the computer screen, "say he was the son of Kate Baker and Dr. Angelo Ferrano, two incredibly remarkable people; he wouldn't be any less incredible than they were.''

"Foo!" she said. "Even if he was their son, they all were as screwed up as they come." And then, in the same breath, she added, "I think I'll go to Portland. I know a few people there and I think I'll take a walk along Waterfront Park. I've been in hiding for too long, and now I need some air.''

"As soon as I go through this, I'll see what I can do to help you on your way.''

Each time he found a file that might interest him, he copied it onto a blank disk from a box next to the computer. Nora would mind, but he didn't care. A woman so quick to condemn the Bakers seemed to have conveniently forgotten her part in the scheme to wrest the Baker fortune from the terms of Kate's will. If they were as screwed up as she said, she belonged to the same club.

It was still well before closing when he had all the information he could find on disk. He shut everything down and locked the door to the records room behind him. Nora was waiting for him. He promised to follow her home so she could pack, and then he promised to follow her to the freeway to make sure she got safely started on her way. She locked her office and told her assistant to close up the museum that afternoon.

NINETEEN

HE WAITED IN the hallway of the house with his back pressed against the wall. He planned for it to be quick and simple. Yes, there would be that satisfying moment of surprise, and then that unbelievable moment of recognition, and then it would be over. Nora Ryan would be dead, one less loose end to worry about.

She'd be getting home from work at any time. He'd watched her carefully after his last visit to see what she'd do. When she went back to the museum, he knew he owned her. She did take a few more precautions now, but she seemed to have accepted the idea he could get to her any time he wanted. He was sure his visit to the museum reaffirmed that.

Nora would lock up the doors to the museum at 5:00 p.m. She would walk down to the café a few blocks away and eat dinner. Then she'd return for her car and drive home. The only reason she'd be late, as she was this evening, was if she had to stop at the store. That would add about twenty minutes to her schedule. She would walk through the door right around 6:30. She was due now.

As if on cue, he heard footsteps coming up the front walk. For a moment that confused him. He hadn't heard the car come up the drive, but then he remembered that she sometimes parked on the street if she planned to go out again. Well, no need for that, Nora, he thought. You won't be going anywhere again.

He strained to hear. It might not be Nora at all. Someone might be coming to see her. He glanced back to make sure the bathroom door had stayed open. He could be through the door and out the bathroom window, which he had left open, in seconds. How fast he went depended on the next few seconds. If Nora was having company, he couldn't risk killing her now—he'd have to kill the guest, too. Killing Nora would cause a certain amount of outrage, but killing a second person, someone he did not know, was too risky. Killing the wrong person might make it so hot for him in the valley that he'd have to give up his search for the gold.

That wasn't an option. He had always filed the gold away as a retirement plan, and as a result he had lived a good life without it. Unfortunately, good lives came to an end. He was getting older. He always knew he couldn't stay in the business forever, but now he was out sooner than he'd expected. He needed the gold.

He heard the key slip into the front lock and then the door open. He smiled. The door shut and Nora's light footsteps moved across the room. He counted a half a dozen steps before he suddenly whirled through the doorway and leveled the gun at the woman, saying as he did, "I'm afraid it's time to say goodbye, Nora."

That was when everything went wrong. When he saw that it wasn't Nora, his finger froze on the trigger while he tried to decide what to do. The woman did not hesitate. She dove to the floor, screaming at the top of her lungs. He swung the gun around to shut up the woman the quickest way he knew: with a bullet to the brain. But that didn't happen, either. Before he could line up a shot at the woman who was scrambling across the floor toward the kitchen, the front door suddenly flew open and the cop from across the street came barging in with his gun drawn.

He didn't get a shot off before a bullet slammed into the wall near his head. He didn't hesitate; he spun back into the hallway and dashed into the bathroom. Two more bullets plowed into the wall in the hallway. He bolted the bathroom door to get a little more time and nearly paid a price for it. Two more bullets cut through the door, just missing his head.

In a fluid motion that would have surprised anyone if they'd known his age, he leaped onto the edge of the bathtub and dove through the open window, executing a somersault in mid-air so that he rolled onto the lawn and came up on his feet in a full stride. He needed every bit of his athleticism because behind him he could hear the bathroom door splintering as it was kicked open. He weaved his way across the lawn and up into the trees behind the house. Three more shots followed. He could hear the bullets whack into the trunks of trees within inches of him.

He was a good shot for a small-time cop. A damned good shot. He probably didn't have anything better to do than spend hours on the pistol range, he thought, as he sprinted up the hill and over the ridge, out of immediate danger, but still in deep trouble. He kept up the sprint until he reached his car parked on the logging road. He started it up and the engine roared to life.

He ran back to his car. Once inside, he slammed the car in gear and pushed the gas pedal to the floor. Once the car lurched forward and started to pick up speed, he stood on the brake, and cranked the steering wheel around. The car did a perfect 180, easily sliding on the dirt road. He lifted his foot from the brake and floored the gas pedal again. The car rocketed its way up the logging road.

He wasn't stupid enough to head back to the main road. The cop was in uniform, complete with one of those little mikes stuck on his shoulder. Cop cars would already be rolling. He wasn't too concerned. He'd traveled the length of the logging road, noting each of the other roads that branched off. In ten minutes he'd have completely circumvented Jacksonville and in another ten would be coming out of the woods north of town near the Applegate River. He'd take the long way around to get back to his motel, avoiding Jacksonville completely.

This time everything went as planned. He never saw a cop car the whole time, even when he returned to the highway. Finally he had time to relax and try to figure out what had happened. Obviously it hadn't been Nora who'd walked into the house. It had been the cop's wife, and the cop had been waiting outside for her.

At least he had done one thing right. If he had shot the woman, he'd never have been able to stay in the valley. That meant coming back some time down the road, after everyone thought he was long gone. Unfortunately, he didn't have the kind of money he needed to wait that long.

And he had learned something else. He'd been sucking air badly by the time he'd reached the car. He wasn't in the kind of shape he was used to being in all his life. The funny part about that was he was working harder now to stay in shape, only his body wasn't coming around. He had pushed himself so hard for so many years, he seemed to have used up some kind of a reserve. For a moment the idea that age was catching up with him passed through his mind, but he dismissed it immediately. He just needed to work harder and eat better. In no time he'd get it all back.

If he hadn't been so absorbed in his physical condition, he might have glanced at the freeway's north-bound lanes when he turned onto it. If he had, he would've seen Nora Ryan's car flash by as she headed for Portland.

IN HER CAR, Nora was going through a mental checklist. After going home for her things, followed faithfully by Paul Fischer in his little sports car, she had returned to the museum to leave an extensive list of things for her replacement to do while she was gone. She ran down the list in her head, making sure she hadn't forgotten anything.

Once done with that list, she ran down the list of things for the house. Yes, she had called to have the newspaper stopped. Instead of giving a forwarding address, she called the post office and asked to have her mail held until she got back. Of course there were no plants or pets to worry about. And, almost as an afterthought, she had called her neighbors and invited them to go over and take whatever fresh food they could find from the refrigerator. They did have a key, and there was no reason to let the food go to waste. Besides, that was just the kind of offer they'd appreciate.

AT THAT MOMENT, Paul Fischer turned the Alfa down the drive to the Baker house. He had followed Nora's car until she'd turned safely onto the freeway. He reached the heavy iron gates that towered above the car. He had just stopped the car when a guard stepped out from behind one of the thick, brick gateposts. Another guard stepped out from behind the post on the other side. This one had his hand on the butt of a holstered gun.

"Can I help you?" the first guard asked.

"I'm Paul Fischer. Pam Livingston is expecting me."

"Would you please get out of the car and come to the gate so we can see some ID?"

As Paul climbed out of the car, both guards stepped back a bit so his view was almost completely blocked by the gateposts. Pam had apparently taken his advice and then some. These guys were very good. He handed his wallet through the fence with his various pieces of identification, including a driver's license and faculty card that contained his photo.

The guard looked at the identifications carefully. He folded the wallet closed and took a cell phone from his shirt pocket. He punched in a number, identifying himself when someone on the other end answered and followed that with a complete description of Paul. Apparently satisfied, he disconnected the call and said to Paul, "Sir, I would like you to return to your car and drive it through the gates after I've opened them. I would then like you to pull off the road there to the right and park your car. We'll keep your car keys for you until you're ready to leave."

Paul didn't argue. He guessed if he had, he wouldn't have been invited in, even if Pam said it was okay. He parked the car, gave the guard the keys, and walked up the drive. He remembered how excited he'd been the first time he'd come up this drive and caught sight of the house. It had been impressive. As he'd walked up the drive, seeing the ornate Victorian structure, with the covered carriage port off the dining room doors and beyond that the fence and then open sky, he thought it was as if the beautiful house sat on a cloud.

Of course it didn't. Once he'd gotten closer to the house he'd seen distant hills and mountains at the south end of the valley. But that first impression had remained. He wished he could feel all that again. Now he felt more like a thief slipping back in the night, even more so than when he actually had been a thief slipping back in the night, when he'd hidden the diaries the first time. This time, though, he was stealing something else. He was about to steal from Kate the terms of the will she had left behind. He had promised Pam he would give her the diaries, because now he believed no more damage could be done with her having them than had already been done. He still didn't know if he was doing the right thing, but maybe it was time to put all of this to rest, and the only way that could happen was if Pam could prove she was the rightful heir to the Baker fortune.

TWENTY

PAUL STOOD AT the fence and stared off across the valley, not really seeing the view because he was—lost in thought. Only a few weeks before he had been in another world, the safe haven of academia, finally distanced from his first trip to this valley.

He didn't hear her come up behind him and only knew she was there when she stood beside him. "Hi," she said. "I thought I'd better come out and tell you not to put your hands on the fence. They've wired it to set off an alarm."

"It looks like you've gone all out on the security. What all have you done?"

"You met the guards. Actually, there's just the two of them. They have a van parked in the trees, a mobile monitoring unit, like the one in the house, only on wheels. Anytime someone approaches the property, one of the sensors picks it up. The man in the van then comes out to back up the other security guard, like when you came to the gate."

"How many hours a day?"

"For now, I've got guards twenty-four hours a day, seven days a week. I've contracted for a month, so let's hope our bad guy either gets caught or gives up and goes away. Even the Baker estate can't afford a thousand dollars a day for security for an indefinite period of time."

"I thought the estate was worth millions," he said.

"It is. Right now about seven million is left. That money is invested very conservatively to protect the principle. The interest pays the property taxes, the maintenance, and the upkeep of the estate. The repairs and improvement to the security system has taken a chunk out of that money, and we're now thirty grand more into security on top of that. I was thinking of having the house re-roofed, but now I think I might just wait until next year."

"You make it sound like the money's not even worth having."

She laughed. "Boy, did you read that wrong. I could do wonders with that money."

"And what would you do with it?" He glanced over at her, wanting to see the expression on her face. He expected to see a bit of ecstasy there as she dreamed about the possibilities. Instead, he was surprised to see that she looked perplexed.

"I really don't know," she said. "I've dreamed about turning it into more money, but I really haven't thought what I would do with it."

"No quitting work and living the life of leisure?"

She shook her head. "I'd never thought of quitting work. I like being a lawyer."

"How about long vacations in the Caribbean?"

"I could do that now if I wanted to."

"Okay, build your dream house."

"This is my dream house, but even if I owned it, I'd still keep the house on Shady Lane. I like it there. I could come up here if I needed to get away."

"So the house would remain a monument."

"Yes, except now it would belong to me, as it should."

"And the money would belong to you, as it should?"

She turned to him with a quizzical look, as if she was wondering if he was teasing her. "You've never really understood," she said. "It's like walking into Nora's museum and seeing a piece of your ancestry on display, but you're not allowed to touch it because one of your distant relatives gave away the rights to it. It's not that you want it so much, but what you do want is the right to decide yourself whether or not it stays in the museum. It's the having the right to it being taken away that's so frustrating."

"And why is it frustrating?"

"Because Kate Baker made some arbitrary guesses about the future, and she acted on what she was sure would be the case, that all the Bakers would be as screwed up as she and her family were. I don't think my father was screwed up. He was a national hero and an officer and a gentleman, by all accounts. I don't think I'm all screwed up."

He saved this question for last because he thought the answer would be the most telling, considering what he knew of the sisters. "Why haven't you ever married?"

"Whoa," she said. "There's a low blow. Before I answer that, let me ask you a question. If you knew how your marriage was going to end, would you have gone through with it in the first place?"

The answer to that was easy. He said, "Absolutely. To wish the marriage had never happened would be to wish that my boys didn't exist. My boys are worth the price of a failed marriage."

"Wonderful comeback, counselor," she said, "and I don't think I'd want to run into you in a court of law."

"Your turn to answer."

"First of all, I was too busy to get married. College

and law school will do that to you. Then I clerked, and
after that I was taken into my current law firm, run by
two excellent lawyers, who, unfortunately for me, had
grown old and tired. They wanted more leisure time to
enjoy the fruits of their labor, so they left me with an
incredible workload. I was determined to prove my
worth as a lawyer, which meant years of sixteen-hour
days, seven days a week.''

"Everyone needs to take time out for love.''

"I took time out for an occasional date. You don't
get too many interested suitors when they find they have
to make an appointment two weeks in advance to see
you. Then I bought out my partners, which meant I had
to work a ton to make this my own firm and pay off a
huge debt. When I finally found time to consider marriage, I settled on Chuck Owings. He was a workaholic,
too, so it seemed we were meant for each other. And
then you came along and showed me otherwise.''

"So I'm the reason you never married?''

"No, you're the reason I didn't marry Chuck Owings.''

"And, in the future?''

"Are you proposing?''

He laughed because he hadn't even considered the
idea. "I wasn't planning on it for the moment.''

"Good, because the answer would be no. When I
know for sure the right guy has come along, I'll consider
marriage.''

"And I'm not the right guy.'' It didn't hurt saying
that. He had managed so far to keep himself from getting
too emotionally involved with Pam.

"No,'' she said with an impish smile on her face,
"I'm not sure yet if you're the right guy.''

"Fair enough,'' he said. He didn't add that he wasn't

sure either if she was the right woman, or that once she had the Baker fortune in hand if either one of them would be interested in the other. "Now, I want you to come over here." He took her by the hand and led her into the enclosure where the Bakers were buried. He stopped them in front of Kate's marker.

"I've seen this before," she said.

"Yes," he said, "and for the last two years, when you were seeing it, you were standing over the Baker diaries."

She did a very slow look down to her feet. "You buried them—here!"

"I gave them back to Kate," he said.

"By now they must be ruined."

"They weren't when I read through them a couple of days ago. Now, if we can find a trowel, I'll reunite you with your grandmother and her sisters."

A half an hour later, Pam had retreated to Emily's bedroom with the diaries, and Paul stood at the front fence watching the light in the valley fade away to night.

When he went back in the house, it was like walking into an empty space, even though it was still filled with the Baker's furniture and decorations. He stopped off in the den and checked the monitors, seeing the same images the guards saw. Despite all the security, he still didn't feel very safe.

He made one last tour of the downstairs area, making sure the doors were all locked and the alarm system was activated and working. He then climbed the stairs to the second floor. He paused on the landing long enough to note the light filtering under the double doors to the bedroom where Pam was staying. He kept going up. In the attic, he went into the maid's room from where he had made his escape. Both the window and the door had been repaired. The window was now wired with a sensor like the ones on the lower floors.

He shut the door and locked it with a key from the inside. He then pulled the chair away from the tiny desk and braced its back under the doorknob. At the window, he untied the curtains and let them fall closed. From a chest at the end of the bed he pulled out a pillow and a blanket. A few minutes later he was curled up in the dark, listening to the sounds of the house, the same ones that the maids, who had used this room, must have heard. In many ways they were peaceful sounds, and in others he could imagine them to be terrifying. In fact, if it hadn't been for the guards outside, that might just be what he would feel—terrified.

TWENTY-ONE

HE SQUATTED IN the middle of a laurel tree that spread out from its base so he was well hidden in a canopy of leaves. From this vantage point, he could see through the tall iron fence into the Baker estate. He was frustrated by what he had learned.

One guard stayed in a van at all times, undoubtedly monitoring a variety of sensors on the grounds. The other wandered in a random pattern around the estate, staying well back from the fence but using a high-beam light to scan the parameter of the estate.

He recognized junction boxes spaced along the base of the fence that sent signals back to the van. The boxes were spaced so that the areas they controlled overlapped. To take out one box would still leave that spot in the fence monitored. To circumvent the system would mean shutting down all the boxes at the same time, but he was sure they were wired to a variety of circuits—so that was impossible.

He had gone back to the culvert to swim his way back into the estate. He had damned near drowned when he ran into the heavy metal grate that now closed off the culvert on the inside of the fence. Water would get through, but nothing else.

He would have to think of another way to get in. One might be to enter in one of the vehicles, either as a legitimate passenger or hiding in it. That would take some planning.

Another possibility would be to try to bluff his way in as a repairman or deliveryman. That would be tricky, too. The guard would check with Livingston and she'd confirm she wasn't expecting anyone. He might be able to overpower one guard, but with the van located well back from the fence and the other guard inside monitoring, he'd never be able to get to both of them before an alarm went off.

He even thought about tunneling his way in. Unfortunately, his best chance of getting to the house unseen would be at night, but they'd rigged the grounds with motion-sensitive floodlights. The lights would follow him from the fence to the house, alerting everyone around.

Still, he didn't completely abandon the idea of tunneling. He might catch everyone off-guard if he sneaked in during daylight. One way or another, he would get back inside the house and he would get the diaries. None of them were more clever than he, that he did not doubt in the least.

INSIDE THE HOUSE, Paul was wandering around in search of a shower. The Baker women all seemed to be bath fans, he discovered, so he about gave up hope when he found the utility room off the kitchen. In the back of it was a changing room for the help, complete with a single-stall shower.

After his shower, he rummaged around in the huge kitchen, going through the cupboards, double refrigerators, and a large, upright freezer, concluding that breakfast was going to be slim pickings.

That problem was solved for him a few minutes later

when he heard the front doors open and the alarm system turn off. He walked to the entry, expecting to find Pam at the door, but instead he found one of the guards there, helping a woman he had not seen before carry in two large boxes of groceries.

Paul took the box from the woman, introducing himself as he did. "I'm Paul Fischer," he said.

"Thanks, that was getting heavy," she said. "I'm Liz Mendoza, Ms. Livingston's legal secretary. She left me with a shopping list, as you can see. There's fresh pastry in one of the boxes. I'll have some hot coffee in a few minutes if you want to wait."

Women who worked for women, he thought, must have a different code. It was okay for the secretary to make coffee. "That sounds great. Is there anything else to carry in?"

She laughed. "Only about half an office and some more groceries. If you'll help Josh there, I'll have some hot coffee and pastries to reward you with when you're done. Pam said she wanted to set up the office in the parlor. She thought she'd use the dining room to meet with clients as all the monitoring equipment in the den might be a bit distracting."

Paul watched her until she disappeared into the dining room. He had to admire Pam's self-confidence; her secretary was nearly as attractive as she was. Obviously Pam was not worried about the competition. Liz was of medium height with short, black hair that was elaborately curled and cut to accentuate her round face and huge brown eyes. She had a nice complexion, slightly pale, but just right to set off bright eyes. When she smiled, as she'd done several times already, she was a knockout. She reminded him of an oriental doll, even though she was Hispanic, not Asian.

As they walked back down the drive to Liz's car, Josh, the guard, said, "Now there's a looker. And wait until you see how much stuff is in the car needs to be carried in. I'm not suppose to do work like this, but who could say no to her?"

Paul agreed. It would take a tough person to say no to that smile. They made six trips altogether. Liz didn't drive a car, she drove a mini-van complete, with a dolly to use to bring in two, two-drawer filing cabinets, a complete computer system, and several large boxes of supplies.

Liz kept her word. The coffee was excellent, as was the selection of pastries. When he wandered out from the kitchen a little later, Liz had already rearranged the furniture in the parlor, had set up the computer on a reading table and was making a writing desk her own. Surrounded by the Victorian furniture and decorations, the room became a very handsome office indeed, Paul thought.

As Liz sorted through some papers on her desk, she suddenly stopped to hold up a note. "I almost forgot, Mr. Fischer. I have a phone message for you." She handed him the note.

He read the message. It was from the chairman of the English department at Southern Oregon. He asked if Paul might stop by this afternoon for a follow-up interview. He smiled and thanked Liz, and then he strolled out of the house onto the front porch. The message certainly was positive. He wouldn't have been invited back if they weren't interested.

He walked across the lawn to the fence, feeling a little frustrated that he couldn't lean on it to admire the view, but if he did he might give one of the guards a coronary.

He stared out across the valley, smelling the sweet air

of morning and appreciating the warmth of the sun on his face. Kate, who had seen more of the world than most women of her day, came back to this spot to live out her life. The valley was a part of her. He didn't know if it was a part of him. For that reason alone he was tempted to call the department chairman and tell him to forget the interview.

But he didn't. He knew he didn't want to return to the school in New England, and that meant he needed a job someplace else. He couldn't afford to turn down a job offer for now until he was sure he had another one. He'd go back to the university and give them a follow-up interview. If they came back with a job offer right away, he'd ask for time to think it over. Then he'd get on the phone to the other schools where he'd had interviews and use the leverage of one job offer to see if he could get another one. He'd have a better chance of enhancing his career in California than here, so he didn't want to give up on one of those prospects too early.

He returned to the house and made a call to Ashland. He agreed to meet with the department head at one, which just gave him enough time to change into his suit and drive over, stopping for a bit of lunch once he got there.

A half an hour later he was walking to his car, still without seeing Pam. He left a message with the secretary to tell her where he was going and when he'd be back. He'd put off wondering how Pam felt about what she'd learned reading the diaries; he was more than likely not going to like what he found out.

The guard had the gate open by the time he'd warmed up the Alfa and put it in gear. He waved as he passed through the gate, and then he gunned the little sports car up the hill. He looked forward to the drive to Ashland through the winding back roads. He didn't even care that his hair would look a mess by the time he got to the university. A brush and some water would straighten it out, and with the day already warm, he didn't need to worry about it being wet by the time of his interview.

THE MAN WAS too close to the fence to be able to bolt from his hiding place without being seen. He had to crawl his way out, keeping the laurel between himself and the guards. When he was finally far enough away, he broke into a sprint to his car, parked in an abandoned gravel quarry about a half mile from the house.

As he came off the hill, he could just make out the bright sports car in the distance. He could see it turn right, heading west. He threw caution to the wind as he gunned the rental car, a Ford Taurus, and shot down the hill, far exceeding the speed limit. He hoped to catch sight of the sports car before it made a turn at the next intersection. Turning left would take it to Medford; turning right would take it to Jacksonville.

The car was out of sight when he reached the intersection. Without seeing which way it had turned, he could only guess. He turned right. He decided to drive to Jacksonville to see if Nora Ryan was at the museum. He still hadn't figured out what happened at her house, but he suspected she'd tipped off the neighbor about him. If he could get to her at the museum, he would kill her. And then he'd return to the intersection and wait for Fischer to come back, so he could kill him, too.

PAUL PARKED next to Lithia Park and walked across the street to a little indoor/outdoor café that offered an odd collection of food. They had one or two items that were Greek, Mexican, Chinese, and American. All of it was fast food, but well-prepared and tasty. He ordered a sweet and sour chicken on rice and then waited for his order at a table under a covered patio.

He'd decided to have lunch after the interview, afraid that he might do something stupid like dribble part of his meal down the front of his shirt and not notice. He had known a few people who had lost out at job interviews because of such carelessness.

The interview had gone well. This time he met with the head of the department and two other professors who taught English, and joining them was the dean of the liberal arts program and the personnel director. He was sure the first interview had made him a viable candidate; this interview would make him a finalist.

He was a little disappointed when he left. He had hoped for some kind of confirmation that he was still being considered for the job, but they'd simply thanked him and made sure they had a number where he could be reached.

As he ate his lunch, he ran through the questions they'd asked. They wanted to know more about his book; they were curious to know if Southern Oregon was the only place he had applied. They wanted to know about his long-term plans; they wondered why he was choosing the West Coast over the East.

He answered all the questions as honestly as he could. The only one he had trouble with was the one about long-term goals. His life had been so full of disorder that he hadn't done the long-term prioritizing yet. Before his divorce he had known what he wanted to do, go as high as he could in an English department in one of the top East Coast schools, but that didn't seem so important now. He still wanted to teach—he did want the satisfaction of teaching at a reputable school, but he wasn't so picky now where that school might be located.

Paul could teach lower and upper division literature and history courses. That and the fact that he wouldn't have tenure appealed to a number of colleges that had asked him for an interview. There was nothing like replacing a retired, tenured, full professor making $70,000–90,000 a year with an untenured associate professor who would settle for less than $50,000, and that was for a good one.

Paul was a good one. He had worked his way up in a thoughtful manner, teaching at a junior college after he got his BA, and then at a college after he got his masters, and then finally at two universities after he got his Ph.D. He came with good recommendations from each. The fact that he had a number of articles printed in both of his areas, and a biography about a Southern Oregon doctor certainly didn't hurt him at Southern Oregon University. He left the interview feeling good about it, but he wasn't convinced that this was the place he wanted to teach. East Coast prestige still meant something to him, and if he couldn't have that, a couple of universities in California would do. Teaching here, on the career ladder, would be a drop down several rungs.

While Southern Oregon decided whether or not he was good enough for it, he still had to decide if it was good enough for him. It had just recently gone from being a college to being declared a university. It wasn't even close to the best school in the state. Nationally, it had no reputation at all in the areas he could teach. He might feel good if they didn't offer him a job.

As he walked back to his car, he wondered why he didn't feel good. Was he feeling so insecure at the moment that a rejection from this university might be devastating? He hoped not.

He drove back the way he came. He'd just turned back on Hanley Road when suddenly his rearview mirror filled with the front end of a car. The car suddenly disappeared from the rearview mirror and reappeared in the side mirror, moving quickly alongside him.

Paul glanced over just long enough to see a baseball cap pulled low over the eyebrows, very darkly tinted sunglasses, and the gun with the silencer on the end pointed at him. He slammed on the brakes of the Alfa and the other car rocketed ahead.

Paul had seen it done in the movies often enough, but he didn't have a clue how they did it—until now. While the Alfa was sliding in a straight line to a stop, he cranked the steering wheel all the way to the left. The car did a slow 180 and came about, pointing toward a ditch in the opposite direction. He didn't wait to see what the other car was doing. He slammed the Alfa into first and shoved the accelerator to the floor and managed to avoid the ditch and head the car in the right direction.

The Spider wasn't a fast car. It accelerated about as quickly as a Honda Civic, which in its day wasn't bad, but in a pursuit with a modern car, not good enough. That he had created a lot of distance between him and the other car with his maneuver was the one advantage that Paul had.

He didn't have a plan. His first thought was to drive back to Jacksonville, the nearest town, and find the police. Medford was tempting, too, but he quickly decided it was too far. The other car would catch him before he got there.

He settled on going with the strength of the little sports car. Another road led back to the Baker estate, but it was narrow and winding, so he usually didn't take it. He took it now and hoped the car following him wasn't driven by a race-car driver.

It didn't take long to find out. Even after he'd thrown the little car through a half dozen sharp turns, the car behind him was inching closer. Driving very close to the edge of his skill, Paul couldn't keep the other guy from closing up. The one question left was whether or not he could keep ahead of him long enough to get back to the estate. He didn't want to think what it would mean if the answer to that was no.

He knew he wasn't driving the car well. He was diving too deep into the corners and then trying to brake and steer at the same time, a disaster waiting to happen. As a result, the other car had closed up almost behind him before he reached the top of the ridge close to the Baker estate.

He pulled himself together and forced his attention on the corners instead of the car behind him. He saw an immediate improvement at the next corner. He braked hard just before the turn while shifting down at the same time, and then he dove into the apex of the corner, accelerating hard out of the corner, but working the gas just a bit when he felt the movement of the car. The little Alfa didn't go into a smooth drift through the corner: Its stiff suspension would send a tire bouncing in the air when it hit a bump and then slam it back on the asphalt. The car felt like it was floating through turbulence.

Still, he noticed two things immediately: The car responded to the gas pedal so that he could quickly bring it under control by easing up on the gas, and the other car fell back through the curve.

That worked in his favor through a half a dozen

curves, giving him about a dozen car-lengths over the other car. Unfortunately, he didn't think that was going to be good enough. From here on out the road was almost straight back to the drive to the estate. The Alfa couldn't outrun the Ford on a straight, not unless he pushed the little car to its top speed and hoped the other driver wasn't as foolish.

At 110 miles per hour the Alfa began to float on the road, seeming to drift back and forth from side to side, almost out of control. The other car was right behind him and firmly planted on the asphalt.

He didn't understand at first, and then he saw it clearly just as the Ford moved up on his rear bumper: The other driver was trying to nudge the Alfa from behind. At this speed it wouldn't take much to send it flying off the road.

He glanced away from the rearview mirror just in time to see another car come around a bend from the other direction. It took all his concentration to drift the Alfa to the right without losing any speed and get it back to its own lane just as the two cars passed.

He was around the bend still holding the road, but he had dropped twenty miles an hour. He flew through a stop sign without a moment to feel grateful that no one was coming the other way. The Taurus was pressing hard behind him, closing up fast to ram him. He didn't know what to do. To slow down would be asking to be killed.

But that was what he did. He pulled toward the side of the road, indicating with his turn signal he planned to stop. The other car eased back, the driver probably curious, but Paul doubted he was foolish enough to fall for any tricks. Except maybe one. When the car was no

longer directly behind him, Paul locked up the brakes of
the Alfa and fought the steering wheel that tried to break
free from his grip because two wheels were on asphalt
and the other two on gravel. Somehow he kept the car
fairly straight with the rear end just beginning to fishtail
off the road when the Taurus screamed by.

The other car was deep into braking, the rear end up
in the air and hopping down the road. No anti-lock
brakes there, Paul thought, as he gathered the Alfa back
up and accelerated as hard as he could, slamming into
the next gear beyond the redline on the tachometer. The
man was just trying to get out of the car when the Alfa
rushed up, so close to his car that he had to pull the door
shut quickly to keep it from being ripped off. By the
time he got the Ford underway again, the Alfa was far
down the road, already turning into the drive to the estate.

THE MAN PULLED the car off to the side of the road and
did a quick U-turn, driving away rapidly in case Fischer
put a call into the cops. He didn't want to be within
miles of the Baker place in a blue Taurus. The last thing
he needed was to be stopped. He didn't want anyone to
have even the remotest chance of identifying him.

He drove through Jacksonville and turned left, following the Applegate River to the north. He didn't bother
to stop by the museum again. He already knew Nora
Ryan was long gone, in hiding someplace where he was
sure he could find her if he had the time, but he didn't
have the time.

He wasn't angry. He was absolutely emotionless as
he considered all the ways in which he would like to
kill Paul Fischer.

PAUL PULLED UP to the gate and waited for the guard to open it, keeping a sharp eye on the rearview mirror to make sure the other car didn't follow him here, although he thought it would take a crazy man to do that.

As he drove through the gate, the guard said, "Boy, that Alfa smells hot and oily. You must've really given it a workout."

Paul smiled. Something a few minutes ago he thought he'd never do again.

TWENTY-TWO

As Paul walked from his car to the front of the house, Pam came out on the porch to meet him. "I hope you didn't look like that when you had your interview," she said.

He glanced back at the Alfa before he stopped at the bottom of the steps. "I really have to get one of those now that I know how to drive it."

"I'm not talking about your car, I'm talking about your hair. It's a mess."

He sat down on the bottom step. "Come here. I have something to tell you that you're not going to want to hear."

She took it better than he thought she would, but as soon as he had finished telling her about the race back to the house, she insisted on calling the police. A half an hour later he was telling his story again, this time to a detective.

When he'd arrived, Pam introduced him to Greg Thomalson, a veteran cop who'd worked with Pam off and on cases over the years. He was in his forties and a little overweight, and he looked tired. He had the appearance of a man worn down by crime. His face was deeply creased, and his hair was completely gray. Paul would have thought him much older if Pam hadn't mentioned his age when she said he was coming to talk to Paul.

Under the detective's guidance, Paul was able to provide details he wouldn't have thought of on his own. Although he had only a brief glimpse of the driver, he was able to answer some questions about him. He was older instead of younger. He may have spotted a little graying at the temple, or it may have been the shadowed features of he face, but whatever it had been, he put the man over forty.

He also noted that the man was trim. Not skinny. He could tell the difference. He got the impression the man was physically fit, and he was right-handed—at least he'd held the gun with that hand.

Paul even knew a bit about the car beside the color. It was a Ford Taurus. Was he sure? Yes. His ex-wife had one. It was the recent model, so it could only be a year or two old. He'd seen the rear license plate when the car shot by him. He couldn't read the numbers or letters. It looked like mud had been splattered on the plate.

The man had been a good driver. Although Paul had driven with wild abandon up the hill, and he had pushed the Alfa to its limits, the other driver had never been far behind and had caught up with ease. Even if he had a more powerful car, it still would've taken some skill for him to catch up, considering the speeds they were going.

Yes, he had seen the gun. Yes, he was sure there'd been a silencer attached to it. The gun was an automatic, not a revolver. No, he didn't know enough about calibers to guess.

Pam, forever the lawyer, presented a neat outline of what they knew: Paul's office and apartment had been broken into on the East Coast; Nora Ryan's office had

been broken into and Nora assaulted; Chuck Owings had
been murdered; Paul had run into the intruder in the
orchard. Nora had been approached twice again, once at
her house and once in the museum. And, as Pam had
learned from the papers, Nora's neighbor had walked in
on an intruder in Nora's house just two days before.

The detective asked, "And you think all of this is tied
to one man?"

Pam didn't hesitate. "Definitely."

"What's the connection, then?" he asked. "What's
he after that ties all of you together?"

"It has something to do with the Bakers," Paul said.
"He stole my research material on the Bakers; he removed material from the museum on the Bakers; he told
Nora Ryan he would leave her alone only if she provided
him with more information on the Bakers; and, he broke
into this house only a few days ago."

"So he's got a thing about the Bakers. Why?"

Paul remained silent. He was curious to hear what
Pam would say to the detective in way of an explanation.
After a moment, she said, "Apparently he thinks that
some of the Baker fortune may still be hidden somewhere: Kate Baker had gold and bonds and even cash
stuffed in half a dozen different places. I believe he
thinks there might be more."

"Any reason he should think that?" Thomalson
asked.

"I think if we knew that," Paul answered, "we might
have a line on who he is. I never ran across anything
that suggested any hidden assets, like gold bullion, in
my research."

The detective went through the house with Pam to
review the security system, and he toured the grounds
with the guards. Before he got in his car to leave, he

said, "If the guy doesn't mind killing, he can get to you. With the security system you have in place, you'll know he's coming, and you can send out an alarm, but he will have time to get to you and get away before we can respond. I don't normally recommend citizens arm themselves, but if you haven't thought about the idea, I suggest you think about it now." He got in his car and drove away.

Paul and Pam were both somber walking back to the house, each thinking about what Thomalson had said. Paul took solace in the fact that killing them wouldn't do much good unless he knew that there was gold for sure, and knew where it was, and he needed to get the two of them out of the way to get to it. Without that knowledge, he would have to hope that either Pam or Paul could provide the clues he needed to find the gold. Which meant he still needed to get to them, if not to kill them, to get information from them.

They walked back to the house and sat on the steps of the porch. "This is the safest place we can be," she said. "The guards are armed and well-trained. Either one of them could stop the man before he got to us. We both have guns." She left it at that. Paul wondered if she was imagining the same kind of wild shoot-out he was imagining. They'd be lucky if they all didn't shoot each other.

"Have you had a chance to check the financial records?" he asked.

"Not yet," she said. "I still need to meet with clients. I have two appointments this afternoon."

"Is that going to be safe?" he asked, thinking the intruder might try anything to get into the house, even posing as a client.

"I'm only seeing old clients. The guards will have them leave their cars outside the gates and Liz will go down to meet them before they can get in. Anyone new will have to deal with one of my new partners.''

That reassured Paul. ''I'll poke around my records again and see if I overlooked anything about the Bakers,'' he said.

''You'll find a couple of boxes full of files in the den, which was all the information I had on the Bakers. Now that I have the diaries, I feel I can share that information with you.''

He was tempted to ask her about the diaries, but he decided that if she wanted him to know her feelings, she would have shared them. He got up. ''I'll be in the den, then, if you need me.''

She nodded, but stayed on the steps while he walked into the house.

Liz had left for the day, but she had been kind enough to leave a full pot of coffee. Paul poured himself a cup and walked to the den with it. He sat in an overstuffed chair next to the fireplace in the den and stared at the boxes on the floor. Most of it he was sure he'd seen before. Pam had gotten some of it from a Hollingsworth descendant, but only after Paul had already arranged to copy the material. Having journeyed through the lives of so many of these people, the Bakers and the Hollingsworths, he wasn't sure he had the energy to travel through them again.

He did have one resource he hadn't tapped yet. He picked up the phone and called Jay McIntire, the last man to spend time with Colonel Baker before he was killed.

It took him awhile to get through. McIntire had retired in Florida. His wife informed Paul that her husband was just now parking the golf cart in the garage.

When McIntire came on the line, Paul explained who

he was and, briefly, that he was in need of some information about Colonel Baker. McIntire didn't hesitate to volunteer information; he said his favorite subject was Colonel O, the man who had given him his life.

After some preliminary sharing of information, Paul finally asked the question he wanted answered. "Did the colonel ever talk about gold?"

"Gold?" McIntire was quiet for some time. When he finally answered, it was after an obvious journey through a very distant time. "You know, he did say something about some gold."

"Do you remember what that was?"

"Give me a minute to think about it. I know it was more an aside than anything, and I know I had been tempted to use it in my book about him."

"But you didn't."

"No."

"You must have had a reason for not using it."

"Yes, yes. I think I remember something about it. The colonel mentioned—and I don't even know what brought it up now—that one of his crazy relatives had once sent him a note about some gold she'd saved for him. I remember him laughing about it at the time."

"Do you remember when this happened?"

"Sometime when he was home on one of his leaves."

"He didn't say who it was who slipped him the note?"

"I don't remember who it was, but I do remember that I thought better of using it in the book for fear I might embarrass a relative."

Paul gave McIntire his number and asked him to call if he thought of anything more.

Emily had to have been the one who sent the note.

What he really needed to know now was, besides the

sisters, who lived or worked at the house who might
have known something about any missing gold. Whoever the man was who was stalking them, supposedly
for the gold, must have heard the story from someone.
That someone had to be Oliver Baker, McIntire, or
someone in the Baker household.

Pam, or more likely Liz, had made the job of going
through the material easy for him. The boxes were par-
titioned by years, and then the files were alphabetized
by names or other categories. Each of the sisters had a
separate file. Financial records were in their own files
for everything from operating expenses to household ex-
penditures. Paul began by going through the files of the
last few years of the sisters' lives.

Three cups of coffee later he knew what he needed to
know. Kate and Emily had a live-in housekeeper during
their declining years, and several other people worked
for them doing maintenance around the house and heavy
cleaning chores.

By the mid-fifties, Kate had leased the unsold Baker
land to neighboring farmers. They worked the land and
paid her a percentage of the profit from it.

Emily did not leave the house except to drive to
church with Kate on Sundays. Kate drove right up until
the time she died. The housekeeper, a Megan O'Rourk,
did all the shopping and managed the additional help.
She lived in the house with the women, actually living
in the room that had at one time been Elizabeth's. Paul
guessed she'd been granted a near-equal status in the
household since she wasn't sent to live in the attic
rooms. He noticed that she'd worked for the women for
twenty years before the sisters died.

He wrote down Megan O'Rourk's name and the
names of the other help on a list. He would plug in his

computer to the phone the next day and see what he could learn about the names on the list from the Internet.

The sun was down by the time he finished. He wandered into the kitchen for something to eat. He found a note on the refrigerator from Pam saying she'd made sandwiches and left some for him inside. Then she'd apparently disappeared back in the bedroom with the diaries.

He took a plate of sandwiches, a bag of chips, and a six-pack of cola back to the den with him. Although the files for the financial records were thick and daunting, he couldn't resist the temptation. He set up a spread sheet on his computer, and then started going through the records, creating categories in his computer for the information he sorted through. Just as he didn't notice the sun go down while he was searching the records, he didn't notice it start to come back up as he continued to enter information.

He'd just finished entering the financial data when a light tap at the door interrupted him. He got up and opened the study door to find Liz standing there with two cups of coffee. "Hi," she said. "I heard you rattling computer keys when I came in. You're either up early or working way too late."

He took the coffee from her, and he took time to admire her. She had on a pair of dark gray slacks and a white blouse, accented with a black ribbon tie. The combination was simple and effective. She was nicely shaped and pretty, and the clothes did not distract him from that.

"Come on in," he said. "I guess I've put in an all-nighter."

She laughed. "That five o'clock shadow and the fact

you haven't blinked since you opened the door gave it away.''

''I got fascinated with Kate Baker's finances. She did such a good job of first making the Baker ranch financially successful, and then making huge profits when she began selling it off, that in the end she had a heck of a time trying to get rid of the money.''

''Yes, that's Pam's curse,'' Liz said.

He glanced up, surprised. He wasn't quite sure what Liz might know, but she seemed to know more than he thought. She glanced over the coffee cup folded in her hands and smiled.

''Which curse is that?''

''Do you mean the curse of success, or the curse of beauty, or the curse of money?''

''Is she cursed by all three?'' he asked.

She shrugged. ''I don't think she believes so. But she's always had to work that much harder to prove herself because so many want to credit whatever she has to her name or to her looks.''

''And how has the Baker money cursed her?''

''If Kate had managed to get rid of all of it as she planned, Pam wouldn't have devoted so much energy, so much of her life, to trying to get control of it. In fact, at first, I don't think she gave it a lot of thought. Only after she started earning money of her own did she realize how long and how much work it would take to get to the six or seven million that's just sitting there in the estate.''

Paul hadn't added up the numbers yet, but he was sure the estate's value when Kate died was nowhere near that amount. ''That seems like a pretty high figure,'' he said.

''Oh, I don't think you know most of the details about that money. That housing development below the estate sits on former Baker land. Pam used her power of attorney to sell off the land.''

''Kate wouldn't have approved.''

Liz shrugged again. ''Taxes on the land were starting to eat into the assets of the estate. Kate would have liked it even less if the estate went into receivership because it began to lose money. Pam sold the land and then invested the money wisely. Interest, earnings, and capital gain have more than tripled the assets of the estate. That's very Kate-like, if you ask me.''

''You sound like a very loyal personal secretary.''

''I am loyal to Pam. She's been a good boss and a good friend. And because she has been a good friend, I've agonized over many of the decisions she's made, and like a good friend I've supported her, anyway.''

''Am I one of the decisions you've agonized over?''

She took a deep breath and let it out, looking him in the eye and smiling the whole time. ''You're one of those, as my mother used to call them, 'wait-and-see guys.' Pam likes you well enough, but you're a step she's needed to take to get to the Baker money. She really does want it for herself, but completely on the up-and-up; she believes she has a right to it.''

He nodded. ''If I've learned anything, I've learned that. I gave her the diaries and other materials I had. I think she has enough information to get what she wants now.''

''I know. I spent a good part of yesterday making copies of everything on your disks.'' She lowered the coffee cup; he could see her smile as she asked, ''So what do you get out of it?''

''Are you asking for you or for Pam?''

''She is curious—and so am I. She's waiting for the

other shoe to fall, so to speak. She's waiting to hear what the price is for the diaries.''

"I might want to publish the book I wrote about the Bakers, but beyond that I can't think of a thing. Calm her worry by telling her that I'm not going to propose marriage, or ask for a million bucks. The book is another thing. Kate left this house as a monument to the frustration of her life. I think most people don't understand that. My book would make her legacy clear to everyone.''

Liz stood. "I'll tell Pam that. You're sure you don't want more?''

"I need to get on with my life, and soon. The book would give my credentials a real boost when I'm looking for teaching jobs.''

"I hear you had an interview for a position at Southern Oregon.''

"It's one of the schools where I applied," he said.

"I have a degree from there," she said. "It just got its university status recently, and the administration is working hard to increase its prestige. That's a long way from the party-school image it had when I was growing up.''

"It doesn't sound like a place where I'd want to teach," he said.

She took his empty coffee cup. "I think you should be flattered if they are interested in you. That means they must consider you a good catch and one who could help improve their status." She walked out of the room, saying over her shoulder, "I brought some fresh pastry.''

He watched her walk away, admiring the nice fit of her slacks. He began to wonder if it might not be a bit unhealthy for a single man to be locked away each day with two such attractive women. He began to wonder what Liz's status was. She didn't wear any rings.

When Liz was gone, he returned to his computer. With all the information in place, he ran his spreadsheet and printed it out on the small portable printer that went with his laptop. He reduced the spreadsheet to fit on the standard-sized paper the printer was able to handle. As a result, he ended up with very tiny print. But despite the size of the print, a number finally jumped off a page, a huge amount considering it was a 1950s figure. He could not account for $120,000 of the Baker money.

He put everything away and climbed the stairs to the attic room. He needed some sleep. Only when his mind was fresh would he be able to go back over those numbers to see if he'd made a mistake. If he hadn't, then his next task was to see if he could figure out where the money went.

He did not wake up until late in the afternoon. When he did come down, Liz was just tidying things up for the end of her workday. Pam was in the dining room with a client, Liz told him. As soon as she was done, Pam said she would like to have dinner with him.

Before he went in the kitchen to take his shower, he asked Liz if he could tie into the phone line with his computer to do some research. She told him that would be fine. Calls after five were routed back to the main office where they employed an answering service.

After he had showered, shaved, and changed, he walked back into the kitchen where he found Pam standing over the stove, cooking spaghetti. "There's some salad mixings by the cutting board if you think you can toss a salad," she said.

He found a variety of vegetables to be cut up into the salad. He took out a knife and began to slice a cucumber.

"I haven't seen much of you lately," he said. "I do use deodorant and brush my teeth," he added.

She had her back to him as she talked. "I'm not avoiding you," she said. "I just been taking my time reading the diaries, and I've had my own work to keep up on. You can be a distraction."

Without seeing the look on her face, he didn't know how to take the last statement. "I stayed up last night and ran the Baker's financial records through a spreadsheet. I couldn't account for a hundred and twenty thousand dollars."

"Good," she said. "That's the same a hundred and twenty grand I couldn't find."

He began to cut up several radishes. "You say that without even a tremor in your voice. I'd think that a hundred and twenty thousand might have made you curious."

She stuck her finger in a pan filled with spaghetti sauce and then tasted it. From a small jar next to the stove, she took a pinch of garlic salt and added it to the sauce. "First, let me congratulate you. I didn't know you were both a literature and a math major. But, you have the advantage of having all the numbers neatly compiled for you. You didn't go through the stacks of record books, the boxes of receipts, and the dozen different bankbooks to get to those neat numbers. For over forty years, millions of dollars flowed through the Bakers' hands. On top of that, Kate attempted to get rid of most of it before she died." She pulled the pot of spaghetti from the stove and turned off the burner. "Between the donations and the assets I found stuffed in bank boxes all over town, I just figured the money hadn't been found, or she gave it away to charities and didn't keep any records."

He chopped up half a head of lettuce and put it in a large bowl she set out for him. "Considering how carefully she kept records, I'd be surprised if she didn't have a record for the money someplace."

"I know, I know," she said, stirring the sauce, "I am going to look into it. There's so much money now that I guess a hundred and twenty thousand didn't seem worth the pain of going through all of those records again."

"Have Liz do it, then," he said.

She did glance back at him this time. "Liz has enough to do. Why her?"

"I would think a third party might be a good idea. I think if either one of us had to go through that stuff again, we'd probably miss something simply because we'd be aggravated because we had to do it."

She turned all the way around with her hands on her hips. "I'll have her work at the office tomorrow, where those records are kept, if you'll be my secretary tomorrow. That's the only way I'd make her life miserable with those records."

"Yeah, I could do that," he said.

She turned back to the stove and moved the sauce to keep from burning it. "Liz won't mind too much. She likes you, and she'll have a laugh every time she thinks of you doing her work."

He finished putting the salad together. "After dinner," he said, "I'm going to hook up to the Net to see if I can find out anything about the people who worked for the Bakers when they died."

"After dinner I have some work to do, too. I'll probably do it in my room."

He nodded, expecting that. "That's a comfortable room," he said.

"Very. In fact, if you get tired of sleeping in the attic, my room has a big bed. Big enough for two."

She was standing with her hands on her hips again when he turned around. "I'll make your salad," he said. "I'll act as your secretary. I'll be glad to share your bed. But I just want you to know that I'm not easy."

She burst out laughing. "Of course you are," she said, "and that's one of the things I like about you."

TWENTY-THREE

HE WOKE UP the next morning with Pam's head on his chest, and one of her arms draped over him. Her face was hidden by the short, curly hair that fanned over it. He smiled to himself, thinking that he hoped she didn't drool.

She was naked. The sheet cut an angle from right hip to left thigh. He lifted his head a bit to admire the curve from waist to hip. Her skin was smooth and golden. She had neither fat nor blemishes. In some ways she did not seem real to him because of that.

One breast lay heavy on the flat of his stomach, the weight of her body spreading it into an oval against his skin. She was warm, not hot. He liked the feel of her next to him.

He moved the hair away from her face. He almost hoped to see a twist of her mouth that would make her look silly; anything to mar the perfection. He knew the failing was his. He felt somehow guilty that something so perfect would want to be in bed with him.

Her mouth was not twisted. She slept with complete calm, the features on her face relaxed as if she might be listening to pleasant music with her eyes closed.

The sun had come up only a while before. He knew it was not yet six. Having slept most of the day before, he hadn't needed a full night's sleep, although he'd drifted off easily after they'd made love. He moved his hand up and down her back, enjoying the texture of her skin. He simply took her in: the warmth, the feel, the smell.

He was a bit disturbed. As much as he enjoyed this, he didn't feel even the first gentle rushes of love. He hadn't felt them the first time, either. Then, he'd thought it was because he was still emotionally wrapped up in his wife. Now he did not know why the feelings were missing. Trust, he guessed, might be at the heart of it—Pam had given him lots of reasons not to trust her.

Her eyes opened suddenly. He watched as they slowly focused on him. When she spoke, her hair tickled him. "I hope I don't have a pattern of your chest hairs embossed on my face."

"I don't have that much hair," he said.

"What time is it?"

"Around six."

"What are you doing awake?"

"I was watching you."

"You must be really bored."

"You're nice to look at."

She rolled over on her back. The sheet slipped even farther down, leaving only her lower legs covered. She made no attempt to cover herself. "I'm going back to sleep. Admire, but don't touch."

She did go back to sleep, quickly. He was able to slip out of bed and dress without waking her. He showered and shaved downstairs, and then he fixed himself something to eat. He wouldn't get any fresh pastry today; Liz was working back at the main office, trying to trace the missing money.

He made coffee, and once it was hot, he poured himself a cup and walked outside to the front fence. While he stood there, half sorting through the information he'd gathered about the Baker help and half drifting off to thoughts about Pam, he had no clue that seventy-five yards away the intruder had him lined up in the cross-hairs of a scope attached to a high-powered rifle.

THE MAN LOVINGLY ran his finger up and down along the trigger. Wrapped around the end of the barrel was a silencer he had made himself, one so good that the guards only yards away would never hear the shot. He would like to squeeze off a shot and embed it in Fischer's head.

He had played the same game with the guards. He had lined them up in the scope and caressed the trigger. He didn't pull it, though. To kill them all would only give him a few hours to try to find the information he needed, and then to find the gold. If he failed, he would never be able to come back once the bodies were found.

He thought of tunneling under the fence to get inside the grounds. He could get into the house, grab the diaries and get out again without being detected. Well, he thought he could. The only thing that held him back was the thought that he might not succeed without setting off an alarm. He'd be back to square one. He'd have to kill them all, and he might not find what he needed.

The best he could do was to line each one up in the scope of the gun and imagine the time when he could pull the trigger. He did not know yet what he could do to get to that point, but he knew if he waited long enough, an opportunity would come. Besides, he'd waited over thirty years to come for the gold; he could wait a little longer.

PAUL FROWNED. He was perplexed. Someone suddenly interested in the Baker gold must have just heard about it, but, according to McIntire, whom he had called again, the last time he'd heard about the gold was from Oliver Baker himself, and the colonel hadn't mentioned it in anything he had written that McIntire had researched to write his book.

How else might someone have learned about the gold? he wondered. Someone might have died and left behind some papers that referred to it. That was the premise he'd pursued last night: He figured that one of the people who'd worked for the Bakers must have died recently and a relative must have discovered a reference to the gold in a diary.

That would be an easy start. He had the names. He just needed to see if any of them had died recently.

Two hours later, he disconnected his computer from the phone and knew that answer. He'd found a half dozen names of people who'd worked for the Bakers, either half-time or full-time, in the mid-fifties. Only one, Megan O'Rourk, the housekeeper, had lived into this decade. She'd been with them for years. Earlier in the spring, someone had broken into her Los Angeles apartment and killed her. The apartment had been ransacked. No one was quite sure what had been taken. She had lived alone, an old woman in retirement, visited occasionally by her children, her grandchildren, and her great grandchildren.

Paul returned to the kitchen for a cup of coffee from a pot he'd made earlier and picked up his printouts. As he walked out the back door of the house to the yard, and then around to the graves, he couldn't help but wonder if O'Rourk's death was tied to all this. And, if it was, then whatever information she'd had was obviously not enough to locate the gold—if there was any.

He leaned on the fence at the head of Kate's grave. "You know," he said, "you really managed to leave a mess behind, despite your good intent. I want you to know I've turned the estate over to your granddaughter. With any luck, she'll squander it all and then the Baker fortune will no longer be a problem for anyone."

He looked through the papers he'd printed out. He realized now that his premise could be wrong: Instead of someone finding out about the gold after O'Rourk's death, someone may have gone looking for her, looking for the information, and then killed her when he didn't get the information.

He walked back toward the house. He had another idea: It seemed farfetched, but he wondered if Pam had found any letters that had been sent to the Bakers; that might be the only source of information about the Bakers that he hadn't seen yet.

He tapped on the bedroom door before he turned the knob and walked in. To his surprise, Pam was still asleep, in much the same position she'd been in when he left. He started to close the door quietly and leave when he heard her sleepy voice say, "Okay, now you can touch."

An hour later, he started his day again, taking another shower and then eating lunch instead of breakfast. That was when he finally had a chance to ask Pam about letters.

"Do you have any letters that were sent to the Bakers, other than the ones they wrote to each other?"

She was picking at her food while they sat at the kitchen table. He'd noticed before that she was a light eater, either from habit or conscious effort. That helped to explain how she stayed so trim, that and the fact that she worked out at a health club. He suspected she was eating even less now because she couldn't get to the club to exercise.

"I think there might be some things stuffed in a trunk in the attic, but I don't remember anything of importance. If it was of any value to the estate, I put it into the records I kept at the office."

He guessed that by "valuable," she meant anything that might help her establish a claim to the estate. "Would you mind if I looked through those things?"

"The access to the attic is actually in the closet of the room where you're staying. There's another door inside the closet. I'm not sure what you'll find up there, though. I haven't looked around myself in years."

He was back to having his own room. He had realized this morning that he was in an awkward position: Pam had invited him to stay with her last night, but he wasn't sure if the invitation extended beyond that. If he went back to his own room without saying anything, he might offend her. On the other hand, assuming he was to stay another night might offend her, as well. The confusion only illustrated how tenuous their relationship was.

He wasn't going to worry about it. The easiest way to deal with it was to be direct. "Thank you for last night," he said. "And this morning. You'll probably want me to sleep upstairs tonight so you can get some rest."

She glanced up from her plate. "To be honest," she said, "I don't know what I want. I enjoy your company. I am also self-centered. I've never had a long-term relationship that required dealing with the other person on a daily basis. You're an experiment."

He started to say something, then stopped. He wasn't quite sure what he was supposed to say to that. "So you do want me to sleep upstairs?"

"I think I want you to ask me that again around bed-time."

"We have a very strange relationship," he said. "I can't even begin to define it."

She poked at the remains of a salad on her plate. "This may come as a surprise," she said, "but I've never made love to a man one evening and then again the next morning; men don't get to spend the night with me. Only you and Chuck have known my feelings about being a Baker. Only you have I let back in my life once I ended my relationship with you the first time. You're chalking up lots of firsts in my life. I'm confused by that because I'm not sure what I feel about you."

"That's one more thing we share," he said, "your confusion."

"Good," she said, pushing away from the table. "I'm going to work in the dining room and you get to do the dishes." She paused in the kitchen doorway. "By the way, I caught you looking at Liz yesterday and I felt jealous. That's a first, too. Jealousy is definitely an Elizabeth or an Emily trait, not one of Kate's. I may not be the right woman for you."

He did the dishes and then climbed the stairs. The only light in the attic came from an oval window set high in the peak of the house above the portico below. The area was actually small, the other servant quarters taking up most of the top floor. It was dry and warm in the attic, but not hot. He had expected cobwebs and dust, but found neither. Pam did say she had the house thoroughly cleaned once a year, and that cleaning must have extended to the attic.

What was stored here was of only modest value. He found several picture frames, several boxes of books, and a set of dishes that were very attractive, but not worth much.

There was a larger steamer trunk under the circular window. Opening it, he found a small packet of letters, but little else. Lifting the tray, he found several dresses; he pulled one out and held it up, recognizing it immediately as the one that Kate wore in her portrait, which now hung in the museum in Jackson. She had been smaller than he imagined, much smaller than Pam. He held it to his nose, expecting to smell a bit of dust, a bit of mold, a bit of age; instead, he caught just a hint of perfume. He'd smelled it before, but where? And then he remembered: He'd smelled the same perfume in the museum the first time he'd been there, just when he was about to leave after seeing Kate's picture.

He walked down the stairs, thumbing through the stack of letters, smiling to himself. He felt as if Kate had sent him a message, but he didn't know what it was. She was still, although they had never been alive at the same time, the most remarkable woman he had ever known.

Pam was waiting for him at the bottom of the stairs. "Liz just called. She says she found out something about the missing money. She'll be over this afternoon."

He held up one letter and waved it at Pam. "It's unopened. It's a letter from Megan O'Rourk, and the date on it is two days after Kate died."

TWENTY-FOUR

LIZ LOOKED GOOD, Paul thought, very good indeed, when she walked in the house carrying a large accordion file folder with her. She was wearing a cream-colored blouse and a gray skirt, short enough to display very shapely legs. The smile on her face suggested to him that she knew she looked good.

"Where do you want to look at this?" Liz asked. She held out the file folder.

"Let's go into the dining room," Pam said.

Paul followed the two of them to the next room, admiring them both. As attractive as Liz was, she was still no match for Pam, who had that little edge of beauty, that one mysterious quality that set her apart from the merely attractive. Paul knew he should feel proud that she had chosen him, at least for the moment, to share her bed.

Pam glanced back at him. It took him a second to figure it out, but then he realized she was watching him to see which of the two he was admiring behind their backs. Fortunately, at that moment he was admiring her. He smiled, and she smiled back.

Liz spread out the papers on the table. "The secret is in the notations," she said. "Kate Baker oversaw a lot of transactions, and in later years, most of the dealings were to sell off property and invest the money, or reinvest capital. Just before World War Two, Kate, probably concerned about the stability of currency during a long world conflict, purchased a hundred and twenty thousand dollars in gold bars, each weighing ten pounds.''

Paul automatically began some quick figuring: at $32 an ounce, each bar would have been worth about $5,000. That would have meant something like twenty-four bars. He was sure it would've fit easily in the bottom of the safe, which might explain why she'd had the safe moved up to the house from Silas Baker's office down by the barns.

''I didn't find twenty-four bars of gold weighing ten pounds. I found some gold, but that was mostly in coin, although there were a few smaller bars of one pound and five pounds.''

''How'd you figure this out?'' Paul asked.

She patted him on the shoulder. ''You made it easy,'' she said. ''You gave me the amount of money I was looking for. Eventually I found an exact amount spent for PMG.''

They both looked at her expectantly. ''PMG?'' Pam asked.

''Precious metal, gold. That's how Kate referred to gold in her records. PMG. The order was handled quietly through the Beekman Bank in Jacksonville. Probably because neither she nor the bank wanted anyone to know she had so much gold on hand.''

''At today's prices,'' Pam said, ''that gold would be worth over ten times its original purchase price. Something like fifty-seven thousand dollars a bar.''

''About one point three million,'' Paul said.

''If someone would murder you for the twenty dollars in your wallet, what might they do for one point three million?'' Pam asked, more of herself than anyone.

"They might just kill more than one person." He held up the letter from Megan O'Rourk.

"What's that?" Liz asked.

"It's a letter from the last housekeeper to work for the Bakers. She quit and moved back to her family in San Francisco shortly before Emily died, and the day after the event she describes in her letter. The letter didn't arrive until after both Emily and Kate were dead, so it went unopened all these years. Let me read it to you:

> *'Dear Miss Kate,*
>
> *I know you'll be furious if you aren't already, but I want to assure you that I had nothing to do with it. It was that Emily in one of her cantankerous moods again she was. As soon as you went out the door for that meeting with the lawyers, she had that safe open and she had that gold stacked on the floor.*
>
> *I want you to know it wasn't me who had a thing to do with it except to please the rantings of her, I did. She had me bring it out and put it on the porch, bar by bar, and then she threatened me with a whipping if I so much as glanced out a window to see where she was going with it.*
>
> *I've no clue where she went. Every once in awhile I'd hear her clumping up the steps to get another load, and then she'd disappear for quite awhile. By the time she came back in, she was a sight, filthy she was, and in a state all worn down by the effort. She went right to bed but not before threatening me again.*
>
> *You know I loved you both dearly, but that was too much for me. That Emily has grown nothing but*

*peculiar with age and I couldn't take it any more.
That's why I left so suddenly. I was afraid of what
would happen when you found out about the gold.
Sincerely, Megan O'Rourk'.''*

Liz took the letter from him and read through it again.
When she was done, she asked the question that both
Pam and Paul had asked already. ''So where's Katie's
gold?''

''That's a good question,'' he said.

''I think we're going to need a pot of coffee for this,''
Liz said. ''By the way. I brought some fresh pastry. I
wasn't sure if Paul could get through the day without
some.''

After she left, Pam said, ''She likes you.''

''Is that bad or good?'' he asked.

''She has good taste in men. It's a compliment.''

''Yes it is,'' he said.

She nodded. ''Now, what about the gold?''

That became the topic of conversation for the rest of
the afternoon. It started in the dining room, and then
drifted to the front porch, and then it ended in the kitchen
as the three of them worked together to prepare dinner.
When they returned to the dining room to eat, the conversation continued.

Pam favored the notion that the gold was long gone.
All the out buildings had been torn down and the land
sold off after the sisters' deaths. She figured that if Emily
had hidden the gold in any one of them, it had either
been buried in the rubble and hauled away or found and
secreted away. In any case, she doubted the gold was
still around.

Paul said he couldn't discount the notion that another
person was involved. Emily may have arranged for

someone unseen by Megan to take the gold away. If that were the case, it probably lined the pockets of another family for years after the women died.

"Emily was saving the gold for your father. Unless she'd become completely addled—and by most accounts she was combative, but not senile—she wouldn't have let the gold be stolen. If it went anywhere, it would have gone someplace safe," Liz said.

"But where?"

"It's Friday. I've got nothing planned for the weekend. I'll go home, gather up some old clothes and then we can go on a treasure hunt."

"Can you bring something for me to wear, too?" Pam asked.

"Of course," she said, laughing. "And I'll make sure I look better than you do, which will be a first."

LIZ RETURNED with more groceries and workclothes for both herself and Pam. They sat in the parlor and talked into the evening about their plans to search the property. Although Megan O'Rourk's letter suggested that Emily had taken the gold away from the house, they decided that it was best to look everywhere.

Liz was to go through all the rooms in the house but the attic and the cellar, neither of which she wanted to explore alone. Paul agreed to search those two areas along with all the other structures on the property, including the tool shed and the pumphouse. Pam would wander the grounds to see if she could see anything unusual that might suggest buried gold.

"I doubt that we'll find anything," Pam said. "I don't think there is anyplace inside or outside of this house I haven't been."

Paul didn't expect them to find the gold, either. He

doubted that Emily could have taken it very far on her own, and there just wasn't any spot on the grounds that hadn't been reworked since the death of the sisters. The graves had been dug, the trees around the estate had been thinned to lessen both fire damage and damage from windstorms, and an asphalt drive had been put in, meaning the ground under it had been dug up and a gravel base put in first. Even the topsoil had been Rototilled around the house for new sod. If she had buried the gold, she would have had to bury it fairly shallow. After all, she wasn't a young woman, and she died shortly afterward.

What did that leave? he wondered. "We'll need a metal detector," he said.

"Where do you get one of those?" Pam asked.

"A sporting goods store," Liz suggested.

"We'll search tomorrow, but I think we'll have to send Liz off for a metal detector," Paul said. "I'm pretty sure we're not going to find the gold sticking up out of the ground."

"And if we do find it," Pam said, "I'm going to give a story to the newspaper: I'm going to let them know that we've found the last of the Baker estate, and I'm going to make sure everyone knows the money is safely banked."

Paul understood. She wanted to get a message to the intruder that there was nothing left for him. Maybe it would work, maybe it wouldn't. He might just be one, when disappointed, who took it out on other people. They really wouldn't be safe until the man was caught.

Late in the evening he climbed the stairs to the attic bedroom. Pam and Liz had gone to bed earlier, Pam to her bedroom and Liz to Kate's old room. He hadn't been invited to join Pam in her room, and he had a passing thought that he wouldn't have minded being invited to Liz's bed. He enjoyed the thought for a moment and then dismissed it. He didn't need the complication, and he didn't need a triangle that would probably leave him on the outside and two friends at odds with each other.

He stayed up, going through the information he'd gathered together over the last few days. He was at a loss. It did not appear that the man had learned about the gold from Megan O'Rourk. He had thought that Oliver Baker might have published something himself with the information about the gold in it. Pam had all his personal effects that had been shipped home when he died. Neither in those few things nor in the handful of mementos Pam's mother had kept was there any reference to gold. Another phone call disclosed that McIntire was positive he had never mentioned the gold to anyone.

Paul sat at the desk and tapped the lead of a pencil on a blank piece of paper. Then how? he wondered. How could someone know about it? Megan, Emily, Kate Baker, and McIntire were the only ones who knew about it, unless the colonel had shared the information with someone else. He couldn't know that, except McIntire's recollection of the colonel as being a solitary man, one who rarely shared much about his personal life. That was why he said he remembered the statement, because it was so unlike the colonel to say something about himself.

Paul tapped the pencil quickly. He had assumed that McIntire had heard about the gold when they were escaping through the jungle. But what if it had been someplace else? And if it had been, who else was there?

That was grasping for straws, but what else did he

have? If anyone else had overheard, he or she could have told another thousand people. Trying to trace the information back to one person would be like trying to trace a rumor to its source.

TWENTY-FIVE

FROM HIS SPOT IN the middle of the laurel tree, he knew what they were doing as soon as he saw them nosing around the house. They were looking for the gold. He had returned simply to watch and wait for an opportunity to get to them, but this was almost enough to make him want to come barreling out of hiding to chase them off—or worse. They would not get his gold.

He mumbled to himself as he watched Pam walk the parameter of this fence. "Not there," he said softly. "I've been all around the fence. You won't find a thing." They wouldn't find a thing anywhere on the grounds. He had wandered them freely, easily circumventing the original alarm system before all of this came about. He hadn't gone after the others until he was sure that he couldn't find the gold on his own.

That's when he began to steal everything he could find about the Bakers. He had started at the museum. He discovered Fischer from those records: Fischer had more knowledge than any of the others about the Baker family, its money and land.

The material he had stolen from Fischer back east was the most complete of the lot, but after reading it he realized that Fischer suspected nothing about the gold. If he didn't know about it, he was sure that Livingston didn't know about it, either. She had even less material than Fischer.

He did make it into Livingston's office one night, which almost did him in. He'd gotten out just as the police arrived. He was never sure where or when the silent alarm had been triggered. He had not taken anything with him, sure that even a few papers discovered missing would reveal what he was doing.

Then he was still working on the premise that one of these people knew about the gold. It had been pure luck on his part that he found out two key pieces of information, both from Livingston's office. One, Pam was sure that Fischer had the diaries. Two, he'd learned the names of the help who were working for the Bakers when the last two sisters died.

He hadn't wanted to kill the old woman in San Francisco, but the only way he was going to find out anything was to ask the right questions, and if he had left her alive, then everyone would have known about the gold and that he was after it. She was as close to the gold as he had gotten so far: She had seen it; she had touched it; she had helped carry it from the old safe in the house.

In the end, in her end, he was convinced she didn't know what had happened to it, which took him back to Jacksonville and Nora Ryan. That old woman had been too clever for her own good, almost getting killed when she caught him in the records room. Some second instinct must have drawn her back to the room, because he was sure he had not made a noise.

She had been clever enough to get out of town, too, and he hadn't tracked her yet. He was running out of sources of information. He hadn't expected to get much from Owings. If anything, he had killed him to keep him from suddenly rushing back in the scene to rescue Livingston. Owings in charge of a police investigation had worried him. Everything he had learned about the man said he was good at what he did. He was pretty sure that Owings had been the only one in the group who could catch him.

He watched Pam and Paul with little interest. They were covering again the same territory he had been over a dozen times. He paid more attention to the secretary as he caught sight of her occasionally as she swept past a window. The other two showed no signs of leaving the grounds, but the secretary, at least until last night, had left each day. When she left the next time, he would follow her and find out what they were up to. Of course he would have to kill her afterward, but that meant little to him. She wasn't his type.

PAUL CLIMBED the stairs that led from the cellar door back up to ground level. The cellar could only be reached from outside the house. It had been used at one time to store dry goods over the winter. Now it was completely empty. The ground was packed down solid under the house. They would need the metal detector for down there. The ground was so solid that he couldn't even probe it with a coat hanger he had taken down with him, untwisted, and used as a rod.

He glanced through the windows and saw Liz inside, carefully examining each panel in the room, tapping to see if anything behind them might be hollow. Last night had been an unusual experience. Unable to sleep, Liz showed up in his room late that night. He had been afraid that he might find himself in an uncomfortable triangle, but it hadn't been that way at all. Liz had sat on the bed with her feet curled up under her, but she had not sent out a single signal that said she expected anything but conversation. And that had made the evening special. He had relaxed and they had visited pleasantly, filling each other in on the other's life.

She was single. She had almost gotten to the altar once, but she knew the guy was right for her in every way but one: She didn't love him. She suspected she might end up single all her life because she wanted everything in a relationship with a man, and she wouldn't settle for less.

He told her he wasn't sure what he wanted. His divorce had been shattering in many ways because he had reached complacency in his marriage and had no longer given any thought to what he wanted from the relationship. Now he knew that a relationship had to be continually reevaluated to keep it fresh.

They had separated knowing a lot more about each other, and they had gone to their own beds without either tension or frustration. He found that remarkable. He didn't think he had ever had a relationship with an available woman who didn't have a hint of sex to it. He certainly had one with Pam.

They met on the front steps, knowing no more than they had before. Each reported what they had found, which had a similar theme: nothing. "We need the metal detector," Paul said. "We could kill ourselves trying to turn over the dirt up here, and I sure don't want to do that unless I'm sure there's something worth digging for."

"You wouldn't have to dig too deep," Pam said. "Silas built the house on this ledge because it was a rocky formation. If the soil had been good, he would have planted something on it. When I had the grounds replanted, I had to bring in topsoil because what was here was either too nutrient-poor or too eroded away."

"Your landscapers didn't find a million dollars in gold, did they?" Paul asked.

"If they did, they've done a really good job of hiding it, considering they did the work ten years ago, and they're still working their tails off trying to make a living."

"No Ferraris or trips to Europe?"

"Since I do their legal work for them, I can safely say no to that."

"I'll go get a medal detector," Liz said.

"Use the law firm's credit card," Pam said.

Liz laughed, a sound that was low, pleasant and real, Paul noticed. "I wouldn't think of paying for it myself. I haven't got much use for one that I can think of."

She went into the house to get her purse. After she was out of sight, Pam said, "I thought you might volunteer to go with her."

"I'm not sure I'm ready for another race through the hills," he said, and then he picked up the drift of her comment. "You must have heard Liz going upstairs last night."

"Old house, creaky stairs."

"She couldn't sleep. We had a good visit. I found out a lot about her. She found out some about me. We didn't make love."

Pam pushed herself up from the steps and walked toward the graves. "I wasn't accusing you," she said, not looking back. "You're both free to do what you want."

He was forced to follow her to continue the conversation. He joined her next to Kate's grave.

"When all of this is over, we'll need to talk," he said. "I assume that because we keep jumping in bed with each other, that we do have something between us. Whatever it is, though, is not good without definition.

You need to know what you want; I need to know what I want. We were miles apart once before. We may be miles apart once again.''

"Liz likes you," she said.

"I like Liz. I like you. She's completely loyal to you. I think it's great we can all like each other. I'm not sleeping with Liz. I'm not sleeping with you as often as I would like to be.''

She turned and smiled at him. "You're good at saying the right things.''

"I've had lots of women busy whipping me in shape, including these three," he said, gesturing to the graves.

"I think Kate might have fallen in love with you. She was, once worn down by the world, a woman without a lot of ambition. I don't mean that in a negative way. My ambition has always been a barrier to my happiness.''

He thought that was a huge confession on Pam's part. "If you keep thinking up such things on your own, you can save a fortune in counseling sessions.''

Liz shouted to them from the porch. "I shouldn't be more than an hour.'' She skipped down the steps and disappeared around the house.

"She has a good sense of herself," Pam said as she watched Liz disappear. "That's what I've always liked about her. She could go up to your room in the middle of the night and not worry about climbing in bed with you. Not that it might not happen, but she knows enough about herself to know that it won't happen if she doesn't want it to. I have some of that in me, but I've been more willing to compromise what I have for what I might get.''

He didn't pursue the thought. He really didn't want a microscopic look at their relationship, examining the pleasures of it against the self-interest. That's what was so difficult about it. No matter how good it felt at any moment, there was always the Bakers' hidden agenda and fortune beneath it.

He walked from the graves to the fence, putting distance between them to put distance between their conversation. He stared off to the west, enjoying again the sun-filled valley, the usual summer fare of hot and dry. Off to the left, he saw Liz's car after it had come down off the hills and headed for Hanley Road. Then he saw the other car. It wasn't the one that had chased him, but there was something about it that was familiar. It looked like another rental car.

That wasn't reason enough to panic, but he decided to go with instinct. "Where's Liz going to get the metal detector?" he asked.

Pam walked away from the graves toward him. "There's a surplus store in Eagle Point. She called them this morning and they said they had one. It's right downtown on the main street."

"I think I am going to drive over there," he said, trying to sound casual. He didn't need to panic both of them over something that might be nothing.

Pam was too sensitive to him. She caught the concern in his voice immediately. "What's wrong?"

"Maybe nothing," he said. "I saw a car behind Liz's. I just got a feeling."

"I'll call the police," she said.

"I'll see if I can catch up with her."

The guard had the gate open by the time he got the Alfa started and warmed up a bit. He gave the man a nod as he drove through. He fought back the urge to panic, driving quickly but not out of control, as he followed Liz.

He found the store easily. It was one of a couple of

dozen in a mall that formed a U around a giant parking lot. He even found her car a dozen rows away from the store. And three spaces down from it was the car that had followed her—empty. He stopped the Alfa in front of the other car. He got out and cautiously looked around the car, finally making a note of the license number before getting back in his car.

He didn't park his car; instead, he drove the Alfa right up to the front of the store and waited for Liz to emerge. She did, but only after enough people had walked by giving him so many dirty looks he was tempted to move on and find a parking space. When she came out of the store, she nearly missed him, the box with the metal detector large enough to block her view.

He called out to her. She lowered the box enough to see over it and nearly stumbled into his car. "I don't think you're suppose to park here," she said.

"Squeeze that thing in behind the seats and hop in."

It was then that she realized he shouldn't be there at all. "What's going on?"

"I saw a car following you as you came down the hill. The car is parked not far from yours. I think you had better go back with me."

"I know it's not the most impressive car in the world, but it is mine—and it's paid for. I don't want to leave it here."

"Have you got someone who can come and get it?"

"My brother has a spare set of keys for it."

"Then I think you should come back with me. He can drive it up to the house and get you. But right now, I think we need to get out of here."

She hesitated with her hand on the door, not quite sure what she should do. Neither she nor Paul noticed the man in the Hallmark Shop, partly hidden by a rack of

greeting cards, watching them intently. He too was trying to decide what to do. The pistol with the silencer on
it was tucked in the back of his pants, hidden under his
light jacket. One bullet from the gun could rupture the
gas tank of a nearby car. With any luck he'd get an
explosion. In the few seconds of confusion afterward, he
could kill both Fischer and the secretary. Chances were
no one would notice.

He moved toward the door.

Liz glanced around. She didn't know a lot about what
was going on. Pam hadn't told her much except that
someone was trying to get information on the Bakers
and the person was willing to use force to get it. The
look of urgency on Paul's face and the uneasy feeling
she had while driving to the store were enough for her
to make a decision. She opened the door to the Alfa and
hopped in.

Paul was already moving before the door shut. The
longer he had sat in the car, the more sure he was the
man was watching him. He'd looked around as much as
he dared, using both the side mirror and the rearview
mirror to see what he could see. The mall was full of
too many people. He saw a dozen men he suspected.

THE MAN WAS OUT the door and on his way back to his
car as soon as he saw the Alfa move. Fischer was on
the move again, and this time he had a head start. The
Alfa had given him enough trouble the last time, even
though it was a much less powerful car than his rental.

PAUL DROVE quickly again, feeling more comfortable
and confident in the car now. The route back was fairly
straight. He knew he wouldn't have an advantage in

a race back to the house, but he didn't push the little sports car.

"Shouldn't you be going a little faster?" Liz asked, twisting around to see if they were being followed.

"I don't want to get a ticket," he said. "If we get stopped, that might give the guy time to get ahead of us."

"I'm more worried about him getting behind us."

"Don't be," he said, reaching a hand into his right pants pocket. He lifted out two objects and dropped them into the palm of her hand.

"What are these?"

"Those are the valves from the rear tires of the car that was following you."

"You're sure the car was following me and not just going to the same place?"

He laughed. "I sure hope so."

HE DIDN'T PAUSE as he walked by his car and saw the two flat tires. The first thing he did was walk over to the secretary's car, make sure no one was looking, and then cut each tire with the blade of a penknife he carried in his pocket.

He walked from there to a bus stop. He would get a ride to the airport and rent another car. The one he left in the parking lot had been rented out of town and charged to a phony credit card. He'd never driven the car without wearing gloves. There was nothing in it that could be traced back to him.

He was angry in the way he always got angry: he turned cold and calculating. If anything his blood pressure went down instead of up. He had been trained as a sniper in the Green Berets. He had spent over thirty years of his life living off the skills he had learned as a soldier in a dozen different places: Vietnam, Panama, Grenada, Kuwait… He was used to pressure and he was used to danger. He was not used to being thwarted. This time, though, he felt it was to his advantage. He now knew what he was going to do: get another car, go back to his motel and pack, collect his other weapons, and then head back to the Baker house. He'd give them the rest of the day to look for the gold, and, whether they found it or not, he'd go in at night and kill them all. He'd save Fischer for last, making sure he died a nasty death, the kind that years of training and combat had taught him to inflict.

TWENTY-SIX

PAUL WASN'T SATISFIED with simply letting it go this time. They'd gotten a call from the Eagle Point police telling them about the four slashed tires on Liz's car. Paul felt so guilty about it he arranged with a local tire place to come out to the mall to put new tires on the car at his expense. Liz promised to reimburse him whatever her insurance company paid her.

That settled, he insisted that Pam call the police again and have them come up to the house to look around the grounds. Since the man had followed Liz, Paul reasoned he must have been watching the house. They needed to do something to discourage him.

While the two women worked the metal detector, Paul, one of the security guards, and two deputy sheriffs, walked around the outside of the fence surrounding the property, exploring well back into the woods. Paul was the first one to notice the laurel tree. He might have missed it all together, but on the side away from the house the ground had been worn away where the intruder crawled into the base of the tree. A deputy went in, emerging a few minutes later with bag filled with assorted litter.

"Our man has a sweet tooth," he said, holding up the bag. "We might get lucky and get a fingerprint off one of these candy wrappers."

They tracked back from the tree, through the woods, to the quarry where the man had parked his car. The deputies decided to call in a lab truck to have casts taken of the tire tracks.

When Paul returned to the house, he found both women sitting on the front porch drinking lemonade. Although it was only early afternoon, the temperature was already pushing ninety degrees. The valley was known for its streaks of hot temperatures.

"How much ground have you covered?" he asked.

"Not enough," Pam said.

Liz added, "You have to go fairly slowly to get a good reading from this. We did the cellar, and we've done the area in front of the house."

"Find anything?" he asked.

They both laughed. Pam said, "Well, we did have this one big find. We got really excited because it seemed like a lot of metal underground."

"And it was, too," Liz said. "We tracked it all the way back to the water faucet on the front of the porch." She pointed to the detector lying on the ground near their feet. "Your turn."

"I'll get to it in a few minutes. I still need to call McIntire again to see if he can remember anyone being present when the colonel was telling him about Emily and the gold. I know it's a long shot, but I can't think of anything else. None of the other ideas have panned out."

"I think he's just trying to get out of doing this," Liz said, "and I think it was his idea."

"Why don't you ladies do a little more, and then I'll be out after I make the call."

Paul emerged back outside with his own glass of lem-onade a half an hour later. Both women were now sitting

on the grass near the front fence, catching some sunshine. He wandered over to them. "I figured I've stalled
as long as I could."

"What did you find out?"

"I found out that old warriors have fading memories.
McIntire wants to check his diary to see if he wrote
anything down. He knows there were others present, but
he doesn't remember if it was a few or a room full of
people."

"That does us a lot of good," Pam said. "You take
over this thing and we'll go make lunch."

Paul didn't expect to find anything. He believed that
240 pounds of gold transported by an old woman alone
couldn't have traveled far and couldn't have been hidden
very well, even if Emily had been the clever manipulator
in the family. Even this exceeded her abilities. His best
guess was that the gold had been found long ago, perhaps even by Kate when she got home that evening. She
could have done just about anything with it, given her
attitude that the Baker fortune was the family pariah.

If it hadn't been Kate, then it could have been any
number of workers contracted out over the years to do
work on the house or grounds. He doubted that any man
in his right mind would simply hand the gold over to a
bunch of lawyers, considering there was no one else who
survived who apparently had a claim to the estate.
Sweating and sweeping the metal detector near the face
of the dam, he was convinced that this was a futile and
wasted search—until the detector starting making a major racket.

He looked at it, dumbfounded. The water behind the
dam couldn't be more than six feet deep, and the water
in front of the dam came out in a trickle that just kept
the creek bed damp.

The noise was persistent enough to bring the women rushing out of the house. "Has he found the gold?" Liz asked of Pam as they hurried over to him.

"No," Pam said, seeing where he was and laughing, "I believe he's found the dam."

"I don't know what I've found," Paul said.

"Certainly you remember the dam," Pam said.

"Yes," he said, not comprehending at first. Then it dawned on him. "Oh, yes, the dam. Silas's dam."

"The one that killed him."

Liz looked back and forth between them. "I think I missed something."

"Great-grandpa Silas"—she turned and winked at Paul, letting him know how far along she'd gotten in the diaries—"would climb the face of the dam when it was time to irrigate in the summer, and turn that wheel on top to lift a gate below to let water out of the reservoir. This dam used to hold back water that collected in the ravine behind the house for a half a mile or more. Now though, with all the development, we're lucky to have as much water behind the dam as we do. So much of it has been diverted in other directions."

"How did the dam kill your great-grandfather?" Liz asked.

"One day Silas climbed the face of the dam to let out some water," Paul said. "As he pulled himself up to the top, he came face to face with a rattlesnake. He didn't duck fast enough and the snake nailed him on the neck."

"The irony in that," Pam said, "was that Silas hated snakes. He would spend hours tracking them down and killing them if anyone reported seeing one. He had a huge jar over half full of rattles from the snakes he killed."

"That must have been like his worst fear come true when he was bitten," Liz said.

"He took it stoically. He went to bed and died without complaint, although it is said he ordered the foreman to track down the snake and kill it," Pam said.

"And put the rattles in the jar?" Paul asked.

Pam nodded. "Of course."

"As fascinating as your family is, I think I need to get back at this. Do you think the detector is picking up the rod the wheel is attached to?"

"More likely it's the metal plate," Pam said. "It all still works. Sometimes in the spring when the rain is heavy, we open it more to keep the water from building up behind the dam too quickly. There's no telling after all these years how sound it is. Still, I think you should check it out."

"Me? You want me to climb in that muck and check it out?"

The two women exchanged looks. "You can't expect us to do it, can you?" Liz asked.

Paul could, but he was pretty sure he wasn't going to have much luck convincing either of them. He sat on the top of the dam and took of his shoes, socks, and shirt.

He was about to lower himself in the water when Pam asked, "You're not going to take off your pants?"

"No," he said, "I'm not."

"We promise not to look," Liz said.

"Let me tell you from personal experience that I don't believe you." He dropped into the water.

The water was deep enough so that he had to let air out of his lungs to sink into the dark water. Because the dam was no longer used for irrigation, only overflow was run off from the pond. As a result the water had filled with algae and silt. He couldn't see beyond the length of his arm in the water.

He felt along the face of the dam. The only thing he found was what he expected to find: the metal plate. His feet sank into a gooey, muddy mess at the bottom of the pond. The mud was so thick that for a moment he thought he might get his feet caught in it. He kicked his feet hard and pushed to the surface. With his head out of the water, he said, "Yeah, the detector is just picking up the metal plate."

He dried quickly in the hot sun. Once he was able to put his clothes back on, he said, "I'll do this for a little while longer, and then it'll be your turn again." He moved away from the dam and starting sweeping toward the back of the property.

They didn't finish sweeping the grounds until late in the afternoon, and by then they were all hungry. Paul climbed the steps of the porch with the metal detector in hand, having taken the final turn at searching the property.

Pam kept dinner simple. There was a tossed salad, bread, and a large bowl of spaghetti on the dining room table. As Paul and Liz walked in, she said, "I had planned steak and lobster for dinner, but only if you found the gold."

"We would've needed the gold to pay for steak and lobster," Paul said.

Once they were seated, Pam asked, "What's next?"

"We walk around the perimeter of the property, shouting 'there is no gold—go away,' as loud as we can," said Paul.

"And after that?"

Paul thought of lots of things he might say. Like, "Go cash in on the estate, Pam, and have a nice life." Or,

"You'll have to do with just a little less money." He checked himself. He had no reason to be mad at Pam. The gold was a whole other thing that neither one of them had foreseen. He hated to think that all of them had been put through this for no reason, especially Chuck and Mrs. O'Rourk.

"I suppose we could extend the search. The estate was much larger than this in the fifties. The gold could be outside the fence."

"That's a good idea," she said. "I'll hire the security service to do the checking, though. I think we've been in enough danger as it is."

"You're being awfully quiet," Paul said to Liz.

She looked up, a strand of spaghetti drooping out of her mouth. With only a little noise, she sucked it in. "First," she said, "I'm hungry. Second, I'm tired. And third, I'm still mad about my tires."

"And I'm tired of the whole thing," Pam said. "I want to sleep in my own bed."

"Move your bed up here," Paul said.

"In my own house," she added.

"Tired of being a Baker already?" he asked.

"I'll always be a Baker and you know it. The place goes with being a Baker, but the more time I spend here the less I like it. I feel like I'm living in a mausoleum."

"What about you?" Liz asked him. "What are you going to do?"

"Go someplace else," he said, without giving it much thought. He glanced up from his plate when the silence extended a bit too long. Both women were looking at him. He would have loved to know what each was thinking at that moment, but they weren't saying, just staring. He added finally, "I don't really know. A lot of what I'll do depends on whether or not I get a job offer. At worst, I go back East. At best I'm in California some-place.''

"California? Yuck!'' Paul had to laugh. Liz's large eyes became huge. She said, ''My family escaped from California. To be Latino in California is to live in a barrio and be stereotyped in servile jobs.''

He managed to keep in the first thought that came to mind. Wasn't working for Pam a form of servitude? "I'm sure California can't be that bad.''

"How many Oregonians migrate down there?'' she asked.

Pam intervened. ''Paul doesn't know that much about our state, or about California, either. Oregonians are a bit independent and proud of their state. They resent it when outsiders come in and try to take it over. At least, that's what they feel about the migration of Californians to Oregon.''

"I know that was true during the eighties when California was hit hard by the recession. I also understand that the trend has changed. The jobs are now back in California and people are moving back in that direction. That's why I had the interviews I did. Colleges in California are having to expand to keep up with the flood of new people.''

"Oh no," Pam said, ''I almost forgot.'' She got up from the table and rushed into the next room. When she returned, she had a sheet of paper. ''McIntire called back. He said to give you this.''

Paul took the paper gratefully. He didn't want to pursue the battle between the States. ''Did he find out anything worthwhile?'' he asked, glancing at the paper.

"Bad news and good news,'' Pam said. ''The bad news is he could remember three other people being present when the colonel mentioned the gold. That exponentially could lead to a lot more people knowing about it. The good news is that two of them are dead. In fact, they were killed in Vietnam where McIntire now remembers the colonel making the statement only a few days before the fateful flight that cost him his life.''

Paul scanned the note. "So only a Corporal Whitehouse was the remaining survivor of those present besides McIntire?''

"Apparently,'' she said.

"Did he say anything more about Whitehouse?''

"Not much. The corporal was assigned to them as an aide.''

"I'll log back on the Internet tonight and go shopping for information. He didn't have the rest of his name?''

"He says he was lucky to remember that. The only reason he knows the name is because he wrote it in his journal. He'd never met anyone named Whitehouse before.''

Paul put the paper down and returned to his meal. "No sense in getting excited about this. There's no telling how many people Whitehouse told the story to about the colonel and his gold.''

WHITEHOUSE, Harold Whitehouse, could have answered that question easily enough. In fact, if Paul had shouted it loud enough, he could have heard it from where they were. Harold Whitehouse knew exactly how many people he had told—none. He had, as he had with many hot tips in his life, filed it away for a time when he could get back to it and see if it panned out. He was back now, dressed in black, including the hood over his head, and he was waiting patiently in some deep grass well back from the fence for the sun to go down. As soon as it turned dark, he would move in and kill them all. The sound of the metal detector going off convinced him of that.

He had watched Fischer make his find at the face of the dam, and he had moved in close enough to hear Pam's explanation. He was sure that it made sense to both of them, but they did not have his experience sweeping fields for mines. A metal grate at the bottom of the dam would cause the detector to make a noise, as long as it was swept back and forth in front of it. But the detector had continued its alarm as Fischer had moved around the face of dam, up to its top, and then again along the bank as he walked to the other side. The detector indicated a lot of metal in the water behind the face of the dam. Harold Whitehouse was sure that it hid at least 240 pounds of it.

TWENTY-SEVEN

PAUL SAT DOWN to his computer, linked again to the Internet, looking for information about a Whitehouse. He found it a frustrating search. He was able to access some military records that were now declassified. He learned that a Whitehouse had stayed in Vietnam for an incredibly long tour, nearly ten years. Only after sorting through military jargon was he able to discover that Whitehouse had been a Green Beret and that at one time he had been classified as a "sniper." A half an hour later he finally linked a Harold Whitehouse to Colonel Baker.

Being a Green Beret, sniper or not, did not explain how that man could move freely in and out of secured areas. Paul guessed that there was a lot more to it than that. Although no one talked about it, he knew that the Green Berets had a small, highly trained corps dedicated to sabotage and even assassination. The Army didn't let soldiers spend as many consecutive tours in Vietnam as Harold had, unless it felt he had special skills it needed.

Paul tried several other tracks. He found and followed Whitehouse's family tree: he was from San Francisco originally. The last of his family had died there.

This was all circumstantial, Paul knew. Whitehouse could have narrated the story of the gold to a thousand people, any one of them the man they had been dealing with. Still, he found it fascinating that Whitehouse's mother had died in San Francisco two weeks before Megan O'Rourk had been killed.

Next, Paul created a very narrow field of search, directed to military archives and aimed specifically at Harold Whitehouse. He didn't expect to get much. What he needed to do was get into current military records, but he didn't know how to do that. Any information about Whitehouse would have to come through sources that stretched beyond the Pentagon.

To his surprise, he struck pay dirt. Harold Whitehouse apparently had a difficult time adjusting to the "new" army, one that embraced an increase of women in its ranks. He had taken the word "embrace" a little too far. He had been court-martialed for sexual harassment of a half a dozen women. Since three of those women were no longer in the military and had civilian attorneys, the case had spread beyond the base where he had been stationed in Alabama.

What Paul found were a series of newspaper articles about the case. From them, he learned that Whitehouse was a career soldier, an instructor in Special Forces who specialized in covert activities, a decorated soldier who had participated in a number of combat situations. He had risen to the rank of Master Sergeant, which was not as high as he could have gone, but a number of questionable episodes in his military career had gotten him busted more than once. Two of those involved fighting, and one another case of harassment.

Whitehouse was found guilty. He was drummed out of the army. The women brought a civil case against him, and the only assets he had of value were his retirement benefits. The court awarded these to the women.

In short, Paul decided, Whitehouse was thrown out of

the army without a penny. The skills he had were lim-
ited, most of them having to do with covert activities,
which Paul imagined had a lot to do with his knowledge
of breaking and entering and probably using some pretty
sophisticated electronic equipment. Under any other circumstances, he might have moved from the military to
government service, but the sexual harassment case was
sure to have made him too great a risk considering the
current political climate. Whitehouse, maybe a little
more than desperate, decided to cash in a chip he had
been holding in reserve for many years: Katie's gold.

Maybe he didn't mean to kill Megan O'Rourk. Re-
gardless, surely he had. And, in the process, he learned
that the gold really existed. Desperate and a murderer,
he apparently felt he had nothing to lose by going after
the gold. Paul was convinced that Harold was their man.

He was now in his fifties. If the man Paul had seen
was Whitehouse, then he knew he was still physically
fit, but perhaps not as wily as he use to be. After all,
Paul had caught him in the act once, Nora Ryan's neighbor had nearly caught him again, and Paul had out-
smarted him in a car chase. He had either had lost his
edge, or he was a desperate man.

He got up from the computer and went upstairs to
Pam's room where the two women had gone to drink
tea. He would tell them about Whitehouse, and then he
would go out and tell the guards what they might be
dealing with. He was sure that wouldn't be very good
news to either of them.

EVEN IF PAUL decided to tell the guards first, he would
have been too late to save the life of one. Harold Whitehouse squeezed off a shot that dropped one of the guards
as he walked along the fence. The man never had

a chance. The rifle was high-powered, complete with a nightscope, silencer, and flash suppresser. It was the most advanced sniper rifle available on the market today. It was, through its evolution, an end product of the kind of rifle that Whitehouse had recommended after years in Vietnam working as a sniper and assassin. Only Harold heard the small *whuff* of noise the rifle made when he fired. The guard had been alive one second and dead the next.

The other guard was in the security trailer. Whitehouse had planned the shot so that the first guard would drop to the ground in an area where the shadows were dark, the line of sight blurred by trees, and the camera angles bad. He was sure the remaining guard had not seen the other one drop, but he was also sure that he would become curious soon enough when the first guard did not emerge back in the light. Everything depended on what would happen in the next few seconds.

If Harold were in the trailer, he knew what he'd do. He would send out an alarm back to his security company, warn the people in the house that something might be up, secure himself in the trailer, and keep watching the monitors for anything suspicious. If he were a college student working a part-time job to earn some money or been given a quick training course and paid low scale, he'd open the trailer door and step out to see what had happened to the other guard.

Whitehouse already knew what the kid inside would do. The security company hired college kids for the night shifts because they were cheap. Good men didn't want to work those kinds of hours, so they got the cushy daytime shifts.

The kid opened the door and stuck his head out, calling out the name of the other guard. That was his last word. Whitehouse had moved himself around for a better view and had a perfect shot when the guard opened the door. He dropped him half in and half out of the trailer.

The next step was a little tricky. Even Harold admitted that they had done a good job of wiring the new security system. He couldn't short out any part of it without setting off an alarm in the house. It had taken him some time, but he had finally found the one weak point. Just outside the fence to the west was a huge cedar tree. It was a stately tree, only slightly deformed along one side where they had cut the branches away from the fence so no one could use a tree limb to drop to the other side.

They had cut it back thirty feet high, but they had either thought that was enough of a drop to discourage someone or they couldn't go higher. The tree still climbed another twenty feet in the air beyond the trimmed area, and one solid limb still hung out over the fence.

Harold left the sniper rifle behind. He checked to make sure he still had the two guns with silencers, four extra clips of ammunition, and a razor-sharp hunting knife. Ten minutes later he was forty feet up the tree and hanging from the branch. He let go of the limb and plunged toward the ground.

He had only been a little off on his calculation. He landed a bit harder than he had expected to, but not hard enough to hurt himself just before the bungee cord pulled him back in the air and then settled him back to earth more softly. He released himself from the harness he had made for the cord and then watch it jerk back up into the night and disappear. He'd have to remember to retrieve it before he left.

He walked cautiously through the shadows, working his way well back from the house until he put the security trailer between him and any view the people inside might have. He wasn't worried. The guards had made it easy for him by leaving the lights on within the compound to make their patrols easier. Once inside, he could move about without worry about setting off alarms. A few moments later he was in the security trailer, carefully going over each of the controls inside. He knew he had about four hours until the next shift came on. He wanted to make sure that he did nothing that would alert someone to a problem up here.

Inside the trailer, he carefully repositioned each of the cameras so that he left a little gap between two of them, a gap big enough for him to walk directly to the house without being seen by someone on one of the monitors inside. He then slipped back outside and worked his way through the shadows from the trailer to the pond behind the dam. There he began to take off his clothes.

BACK IN THE servant's room, Paul took off his shoes as he prepared for bed. He had meant to talk to the guards before he went to bed, but he had gotten into a long, involved conversation with Pam and Liz about what they should or shouldn't do with the information they had about Harold Whitehouse. Paul wanted to take it directly to the police. Pam wanted to turn it over to the district attorney's office. She felt that the police might do something stupid that would drive Whitehouse away. The DA, she assured him, would be far more discreet.

She said, "The last thing I want is for Whitehouse to run. That would mean I'd have to spend the rest of my life worrying about whether or not he'd return."

Paul's own argument was simple enough. "This man is incredibly dangerous. Two men up here are not enough to protect us from him. We need a company of men. Only the police can provide that kind of protection.''

Pam responded, "Tomorrow I'll ask that the security be doubled. I'll talk to the DA and see if we can't get some intensive sheriff's patrols in this area. That will discourage the man from getting too close, and it will give the DA some time to try to track him down.''

When he saw that he wasn't going to win the argument, Paul gave up and climbed the stairs to go to bed. He didn't think about the guards until he was ready to undress. He was under the covers before his instincts got the best of him. The men out there needed to know the danger they faced. He climbed back out of bed and started to dress.

WHITEHOUSE FOUND the first gold bar with his toes. The water behind the dam was just over his head. The bottom of the pond was thick with soft mud. At first he dove under and tried to probe the mud with his hands, but the water kept him too buoyant and he couldn't get any leverage. Next he grabbed the shaft that ran from the wheel on top of the dam to the metal gate below. By holding on to this tightly, he could push his feet deep into the mud. That was when the toes of his right foot found the first bar of gold.

He ducked his head under the water and let out enough air for him to sink to the bottom. By holding onto the shaft underwater with one hand, he had enough leverage to dig down into the mud with his other hand. The gold fought to hang on to the bottom, entombed in the mud below. It took most of his strength to pull the first bar loose. After an hour of this, he had thirteen dark, muddy bars sitting on the bank of the pond when he heard the door to the house open.

PAUL WALKED AROUND to the side of the house and stood on the walk, scanning the darkness to see if he could see the guard who should be patrolling the grounds. He strained to hear some kind of a sound. The only noise he heard came from the direction of the pond, a slight slap of something on water. Although he hadn't seen one before, he wondered if the estate had muskrats living along the banks of the pond.

He started to walk toward the security trailer. He was halfway there when he hesitated. Something wasn't right. He had an uncomfortable feeling. To himself, in a whisper, he said. "All's not right, Kate. What is it?"

He didn't believe in the supernatural. He believed that the dead were dead forever, and they were forever separated from the living. But at that moment, a cool breeze suddenly picked up, so cool that it sent a chill up his back. He didn't need much persuasion. He spun on his heels and dashed back toward the house. He didn't hear the shot fired, but he felt the bullet slip just past his right cheek and he heard it whap into the side of the house.

WHITEHOUSE STOOD, still naked, next to the back of the trailer where he had lined up the perfect shot, center forehead, on Fischer. Just as he squeezed it off, the man had whirled around. The bullet still came close to its mark. He lined up a second shot at the back of Fischer's head. Just as he squeezed off that one, Fischer dove to the ground, did a somersault, and came back up on his feet, zigzagging the last few steps until he disappeared from view.

Now he'd have to do it the hard way. He stepped into the trailer and activated a shunt that would keep an alarm from being sent to the security company. He had already cut the phone line and shut off the electricity in the house. Next, he pulled out a small transmitter, self-contained and self-powered, from the backpack he'd worn when he jumped into the compound. It was something he'd invented himself, and he hoped to use the gold to help market the device. The idea was simple enough, a take-off on the jamming of signals done by the communists in the '50s and '60s.

The device scanned through the frequencies used by a cell phone, sending out a disruptive impulse at each setting. It could transmit about 100 yards, making any cell phone in that radius useless. He had developed the device when cell phones became popular, making it dangerous to break into a place even after cutting the phone line.

PAUL LOCKED the front door and dashed up the stairs, not bothering to knock as he burst into Pam's room. He could see her shoot up in bed, clutching for something nearby. He'd forgotten that she had a gun. "Pam, it's me," he shouted. "Whitehouse is on the grounds. I think the guards are dead."

She struggled to turn on the bedside lamp. He heard the click but nothing happened. She then reached into the drawer of the bedside table and pulled out a flashlight. She turned it on to use it to find the cell phone. Suddenly she flicked the light toward the door.

Liz came in, looking disheveled and frightened. "I heard all this noise—"

Pam called 911 on her cell phone. She listened briefly. Frantically, she turned it off and on again before trying to dial again. "The phone's not working," she said, holding it out to Paul.

He tried it several times. He got the same response. He would hear the sharp note of a number being pushed, and then suddenly the phone would let out a scramble of beeps and shut down. "He must have done something," he said.

"To my cell phone?"

"To the signal." He stuck the phone in his shirt pocket. "Come on. Get our clothes and bring your gun. I want us to move up to the top floor. The windows are secure up there, and he'll have to come up the stairs to get to us." He led the way.

WHITEHOUSE KNEW he had little time left. After setting his jammer to work, he rushed back to the pond and dove in head first. He worked as fast as he could to find the other bars of gold. He was sure that in the house they were grabbing whatever weapons they could find and boarding themselves up, probably in one of the bedrooms.

They could sweat it out a little longer. He would take care of them as soon as he had the gold. Fortunately, old Emily had made it pretty easy for him. She must have just walked across the face of the dam and dropped the bars from the middle, close to the gate. It took him only about a half an hour more to find the rest of the bars.

PAUL HAD JAMMED a chair under the doorknob. He knew that this hadn't worked well before, but he didn't care. This time Whitehouse would have to get in the room, and then open the closet door to get to the attic door. By then they'd have had all the warning they needed about his presence. He'd made a pile of all the things in the attic between them and the door. The barricade would offer them some protection.

He had told Pam the obvious strategy. "If he tries to come through the door, we both empty our guns into him."

WHITEHOUSE FINISHED what he needed to do before he took care of the people in the house. He took the keys for the van used by the security people from the pocket of one of the dead guards. He loaded the gold into the van. He gathered together everything he had brought into the compound with him, sticking the items in the van except for the jammer, which he left sitting on the roof of the truck.

Convinced he had everything from inside the compound, he opened the double gates to the road out, walked into the woods, and rounded up the items he had left outside the fence. He brought these back and put them in the van. After he went into the house, he wouldn't have much time. He'd drive the van to the quarry, transfer the gold and his things into his car, and then run the van into the water that had filled part of the quarry bed. That would create enough confusion, long enough for him to disappear.

THE TENSION IN the attic stretched so taut that Paul was afraid that any one of them might explode. As it was they were dead silent, straining to hear even the slightest sound. When the door opened downstairs, it was like the noise sprung the tension, and all three let out a collective expulsion of held breath.

"He's coming," Liz said, wedging herself behind the other two. They were, after all, the ones with the guns.

They followed the noise he made downstairs as he moved from room to room, testing doorknobs and then swinging open the doors. He didn't seem to care if they heard him or not. He moved in a circle, through the parlor, into the kitchen, to the dining room, then the den, and finally to the staircase. He climbed up the stairs, making less noise now, pausing occasionally, as if he were listening.

He made the same tour of the second floor. Apparently convinced that they were not there, either, he slowly climbed the stairs to the attic rooms. They heard him rattle the doorknob to Paul's room. They held their breath, expecting to hear him crash against the door. Instead, they were stunned to hear laughter.

His voice cut though the walls. "I'd like to finish off this game of ours in the right way, Fischer, but I simply don't have the time. By the way, I found the gold. It was in the pond. Your metal detector wasn't lying to you at all."

"We seem to have a stalemate, Whitehouse," Paul said. "If you try to get in here, we'll kill you."

Whitehouse was quiet for a long time, surprised that Fischer knew his name. He also weighed what was meant by "we." They must have more than one gun. It didn't matter, though. He had no intention of going in. What worried him was whether or not they had given his name to the authorities. He shrugged it off. He had other identities he could use. They wouldn't find him again.

"I thought Owings was the clever one, the one I should worry about. You, though, Fischer, have been very resourceful. I'm truly sorry I didn't kill you before this."

Paul yelled back, "I'd take the gold and run as fast as you can. Who knows? You might get away."

A metallic noise snapped in the night. "Do you know what that was, Fischer?"

"The safety on your gun going off, I would guess."

Whitehouse laughed. "You could only wish. That was the pin from an incendiary grenade. I'm about to drop it and run down the stairs. By the time I drive through the gates to this graveyard, you three will be toasted fritters. Have a real painful death." They heard the sound of a *thunk* and then Whitehouse's feet on the stairs.

The initial blast blew the door to the attic off its hinges. It slammed into the barricade they had created. A flash of flames rushed in behind the door. They were protected by the pile they had made, but Paul saw immediately that the blast that had eliminated their escape route.

"Give me your gun," he said to Pam. When she reached it up, he ripped it out of her hand and headed to the circular window. "Drag a trunk over here." While the women did what he told them, he used the butts of both guns, one in each hand, to break out the glass of the window. When they got the trunk over to the window, he stepped up on it. He nearly swung his face up, into a bullet. Under the roar of the flames, he could hear the *thunk* of bullets slamming into the house around the window.

He'd take a bullet over fire any day, he thought. He stood up, stuck one arm through the shattered window and emptied its clip into the yard below, in the direction from which Whitehouse was shooting. He then switched guns and fired the next clip at the van parked near the trailer. He heard glass breaking, metal being ripped, and the sound of air rushing from a tire. "The son of a bitch will have to carry the gold out on his back," he said. And then he realized he was out of bullets.

Whitehouse was still flat on the ground because when he'd dived to the ground to avoid the gunfire he'd wrenched his knee. When the pain hit, he screamed, "Goddamn son of a bitch!" He groped for the gun he dropped when he'd hit the ground, but couldn't find it. It must have flown from his hand. He hobbled toward the truck to get another one.

PAUL COULDN'T SEE HIM clearly, but he could tell that something moved off in the dark toward the truck. He broke out the rest of the windows, swept glass away from the sill, and then pushed himself through it. He eased himself down, hanging from the sill, and then let himself drop.

He fell about ten feet, and landed on the sloped hip roof that lined the second floor. The pitch was enough for his feet to keep sliding down, and he fell a few feet until he landed on the flat roof of the portico. He scrambled back up, encouraged by the orange glow that radiated from the top of the house.

With one foot on the hip roof and the other on the portico roof, he shouted to Pam, "Do what I did and let yourself drop. I'll catch you."

She did as she was told, easing herself through the window and then lowering her body down until she was hanging from her fingertips. When he yelled, "Jump," she dropped down. She landed between his arms, and he shoved his body into her, pinning her to the windows of the back bedroom. She let out a cry of pain.

"You need to get inside," he said. "You'll have to break a pain of glass to open one of the windows."

"I don't have anything to break the glass with," she panted out.

Shit, he thought. He'd dropped the guns on the floor of the attic when they were empty. "Use a shoe," he shouted.

"I wore slippers."

Liz screamed from above. "Help me! The fire is getting too hot."

He patted his pockets, searching, and found the cell phone. He shoved himself up, reaching with one hand to grab the top of the lower window. He then brought the other hand around with the cell phone in it and smashed the glass just below the lock. The pain was incredible. He had sliced his hand on the broken glass. He held tight, thrusting the hand through the hole, dropping the phone, and undoing the lock. The pain was too great; he had to let go, tumbling back onto the portico.

Pam shoved open the window and scramble inside. Just as Paul got to his feet and stepped back to the side of the building, Liz came crashing down on top of him, toppling them both over and back onto the portico roof. He didn't waste a second, again scrambling to his feet while tugging on Liz's arm. He forced her body ahead of him, shoving whatever part of her he could, until she was up against the side of the building. Something slammed into the building near his face. With a final heave that strained every muscle in his body, he shoved Liz through the open window.

He desperately wanted to follow her, but he knew what had hit close to his head: a bullet, one of a much larger caliber than the last. Whitehouse had a rifle this time. Paul guessed he had a night scope on it as well or the bullet wouldn't have been so close. He let himself fall back on the roof where he lay flat on his back, yelling at the women. "Run, damn it, run! Go out the far side of the house."

He was afraid they might look back out of the window at him, giving Whitehouse an easy target. Neither did. The bullet probably went through the wall, he thought.

If it didn't hit Pam, then it scared her enough for her to keep moving.

The whole top of the house was aflame. Century-old timber, dry as desert sand, turned the top floor into a giant torch. The whole valley below would have a spectacular view. That meant help couldn't be far away. He hoped he could stay where he was until the fire and police arrived.

Whitehouse's voice seemed as if it was right next to him when he shouted, "I want the keys to your car, you stupid shithead! One of your dumb-ass lucky shots hit the carburetor on the truck. It won't start."

Now he knew. Whitehouse was directly below him, under the portico. As long as he was there, he wasn't after the women. "Take a flying leap."

His left leg flew in the air as a bullet ripped through the roof and the inside of his thigh as well. His whole body became electric from the shock. It was all he could do to roll over and over away from the spot where he had been shot.

"Throw down the keys or I'll come up to get them."

"I'm throwing them down," Paul said. He dug the keys out of his pocket and tossed them over the back edge of the roof. Two more bullets tore through the roof, neither close this time as Whitehouse moved from under the portico to where the keys had landed.

"It may not be today," he shouted, "but you're dead, Fischer. I promise it."

Suddenly the room where the women had entered flashed into flame. Within seconds, the windows along that side of the house began to bow out as the glass melted. "Oh, Lord," Paul mumbled. He didn't want that coming down on top of him. He was already being showered by flaming debris from above. He dragged himself to the front edge of the portico and lowered himself over. He hung for a long time, trying not to think about the pain he would feel when he hit the ground.

He dropped, doing his best to land on his good leg. The pain was more than he had ever felt before, so intense that he waved in and out of consciousness. He might have given into it and let himself drift off, but suddenly the barrel of a rifle was pointed in his face. Whitehouse whispered fiercely, "You didn't think I'd leave without saying goodbye, did you?"

Here it was, Paul thought. Maybe he would get to meet Kate Baker now.

And then the world came crashing down.

It wasn't the world, but it sounded like it. Part of the upper floor, along with the melted windows, fell onto the portico roof, enough heavy and hot debris to buckle the columns that supported the roof and send parts of the portico itself tumbling down on them. Whitehouse was staggered on his feet. The gun wavered and the bullet plowed into the ground next to Paul's head. He didn't wait for another. He grabbed the barrel of the rifle, yanked the gun from the surprised Whitehouse, and flung it into the burning debris that continued to shower down.

Whitehouse whirled around to find the rifle, grunting in rage as he pulled it from the fire. Paul also grunted, but in pain as he forced himself to his feet and half ran and half hobbled off into the dark toward the front of the house. He didn't look back. He moved as quickly as he could to get as far away from Whitehouse as he could. He knew he only had a few seconds at best.

The scope on the rifle had caught in the debris. Whitehouse had to reach a hand into burning embers to free the gun. By the time he jerked it loose and turned back around, Fischer was gone. He knew it was hopeless now. In the distance he could see a dozen set of flashing lights hurrying along the roads below, heading in the direction of the house. He would have to let the gold go. But he still had enough time to kill Fischer and get away. If killing Fischer was the only satisfaction he was to have, then he'd get that satisfaction.

Paul had wanted to go around the house on the far side, but he was afraid he might lead Whitehouse to Pam and Liz. Instead he stumbled to the little cemetery enclosure and through the iron gate. He would have loved to rip loose one of the iron bars with its spear tip on top to throw at Whitehouse. He stretched flat on the ground in the darkness and prayed that Whitehouse would give up the chase. The prayer got a quick answer—no. He could make out Whitehouse as he came around the corner of the house.

He kept moving around the house, away from Paul. Again Paul was torn. Right now he was safe, but if Whitehouse kept going, he might find the women. He said softly, "I'm here, by the fence."

Whitehouse whirled around and put the rifle to his shoulder, his eye to the night scope. He couldn't see anything. The lens was covered with soot. He moved in the direction of the voice. The light from the fire that had now burned itself down to the bottom floor made the scope unnecessary. Still, he couldn't see Fischer.

Paul hugged Kate Baker's headstone, the shadows protecting him for now from Whitehouse's view. The killer veered away from Paul, obviously staying well back from any shadowed area that might hide him. Paul let him get by, and then when Whitehouse turned away to look down the length of the front fence, he got up from the ground and moved to the man. He hoped to get his hands on the rifle as it swung around, sure that it would swing around, and yank it away from Whitehouse again.

Paul had guessed that the man would whirl to his right. He guessed wrong, Whitehouse whirled all the way around to his left, moving the gun barrel away from his grasp. Paul was caught up short by the cemetery fence. Whitehouse never stopped his swing. He brought the barrel around in a vicious arc that caught Paul on the side of the face. Paul sank slowly to the ground as the world began to dim.

Whitehouse leaned over the fence with the gun pointed at Paul's head. When Paul could focus again, he saw the killer, his image satanic in the glow of the fire, a tight smile on his face. "This time it's goodbye. See you in hell."

Paul acted instinctively, heaving himself up so that he could just stretch out and wrap his hands around the barrel of the gun. Whitehouse laughed and pulled the trigger. Paul's body jerked back violently from the blow to his chest.

Kate Baker was standing there to meet him. She was lovely, dressed in the same gown that she wore for her portrait, now hanging in the museum in Jacksonville. She was lovelier than he had ever seen her before. She reached out a hand to him. He reached out one to her.

And then his eyes snapped open and he saw all of hell he ever wanted to see.

He still had his hands wrapped around the barrel of the gun. Whitehouse still held on to the other end of it, the smile on his face now turned to a grimace. When Paul had been driven backward by the force of the bullet, he had jerked Whitehouse forward with him. Two spear-heads on top of the iron fence were now embedded deep into his gut. The rifle slipped from his fingers and dropped to the ground. His arms and head slowly sank down, until he hung doubled over the top of the low fence.

He raised his head slightly, so he could see Paul. "Why?" he asked.

"This is what happens when you mess with the Bakers," Paul whispered.

Whitehouse glanced toward the graves of the sisters and then his head slowly sank down again as he died.

TWENTY-EIGHT

HE STAYED AWAY as long as he could, ignoring the voices in the far distance that kept trying to draw him back to the real world. They tried all sorts of tricks on him, but the one that finally worked was when some tiny, far-off voice said that his sons were there to see him.

Even then it took a long time to travel the million miles to the tiny voice, so long that when he finally asked where the boys were, the nurse said the boys had already gone because it was late at night.

After that it was a steady stream of doctors and nurses, each prying up a little more the lid he had pulled down tight around him. When the light finally came through so overpowering that he could barely stand it, he was able to ask again, where were his boys? By then it was noon the next day.

The first person he saw who wasn't swathed in white was Pam Livingston. She was several colors, but her face was as pale as the uniforms the others wore.

"You were suppose to die," she said. "They said you'd never make it through another night."

He could do little more than whisper, so he didn't try to do more. "Don't you just hate it when they get it all wrong?"

"They said I only get a few minutes. They say you need to rest."

"That's very thoughtful of 'they,' whoever 'they' are."

"The doctors."

"I have more than one?"

"An army of them. High-powered bullets through the chest do a lot of damage."

"I'm glad I missed it," Paul said. "How long have I been out?"

"Six days."

That didn't surprise him. He knew that he had been in some kind of a netherworld, one full of those distant sounds and distant voices. He even knew that he might not return. Several times he had felt it all fade away almost to the point of extinction. He hadn't been afraid. The fear had come before, in the burning room, on the portico roof, and then, when he had given away his hiding place. He knew then that he might die, and he had felt fear. The bullet had taken away the fear. In those few seconds before he lost consciousness, he felt a strange moment of peace.

"It was a good six days," he said.

For the first time she smiled. "Oh?"

"I spent time with Kate Baker," he whispered.

The smile faded; the concern on her face was back. "If you talk like that," she said, "they'll never let you out."

"It's okay. Kate stayed behind. I came back."

"And how did you and Kate get along?"

"Fine," he said, "but in the end she decided she was too old for me."

Pam kneeled down beside the bed and took one of his

hands in hers. "I bet Kate wasn't very happy about the house."

He tried to squeeze her hand, but he could barely move his fingers. He was very weak, a price worth paying to win a battle with death, he decided. "The house did her little good. When you have eternity to brood about the little life you got, things like houses lose significance. Were they able to save anything?"

"What remains of the house fits nicely into the cellar, and it's still smoldering. It's all gone."

"My boys?" he asked.

"I have them at my house. The doctors say you'll need a few days before you can see them. I'm supposed to be here to reassure you."

"And Beth?"

"If she'd come with the boys, she would have admitted that she still cared."

He accepted that. He would have been more surprised to learn that she was waiting outside.

"Are the boys okay?"

"They've been great. They seemed stunned by the fact that their father is a hero."

"I'm not a hero, but it's certainly a step up from what they were thinking of me earlier this summer."

"You saved two damsels in distress. You killed a very bad guy. The verdict was unanimous: the women you saved, the police, the press; you're a hero."

"I jerked on the barrel of the gun. I probably shot myself because of it."

Pam gently stroked the back of his hand. "We were coming back around to the front of the house," she said, "thinking he would be going back to where the car was. If you hadn't called out to him, he would have walked right into us. You saved our lives."

He was uncomfortable with this. He had called out, and it had been to keep Whitehouse from going in the direction Paul thought the women had gone. He couldn't put a label on it. Hero? Fool? He didn't know. It had all happened so quickly and there had been no time to reason. He just did. By some inexplicable calculation of odds, he had survived, the women had survived, and Whitehouse had died. If you roll the dice often enough, a good number will come up occasionally. He got his lucky roll.

"I'd like to see the boys as soon as I can. Don't let anyone talk you out of bringing them in."

"I'll bring them back this evening. I do want to know one thing, though, before I go. I saw Whitehouse say something to you just before he died. What was it?"

"He asked 'why?'"

"Why?"

"Yes. I guess it was his 'Rosebud.' I will never know what he expected to hear from me. Why had I been the one to out-fox him? Why had his luck run out just when he found the gold? Why then, why there? I don't know what he wanted to hear."

"What did you tell him?"

He smiled weakly. "I'm not sure," he said, "but I know he didn't die laughing."

"It's okay now," she said. "They think you're past the worst of it. You'll stay with me until you're completely recovered, and then you have choices to make. Southern Oregon has offered you a job, and so has one of the schools in California."

"Yes, choices," he said. "I'm sorry about the house. I suppose that will limit your choices now."

"Why's that?"

"The diaries, all the records, were destroyed in the fire. You'll have a tough time making your case."

She stood up, looking very beautiful to him in the bright light of the room, even as pale as she was. "You don't need to worry. After I went through the window, I ran back to my room and gathered up as much as I could, including the diaries. With Liz's help, I got all the important papers out of the fire. I'm afraid your things were destroyed."

If he could laugh, he would have. Pam Livingston looked to get it all. "What will you do about the estate?"

"What is there to do? The house is gone. Taxes on the land aren't bad. I'll keep it. I want the Bakers to rest in peace up there."

So, in the end, Silas Baker got little more than his cemetery plot, Paul thought: Some legacy for a man who lusted for vast stretches of land. Emily would be happy because the Baker fortune would be passed on to a Baker. Elizabeth would root for Pam to have all the things she didn't get out of life. And Kate would be sad because there would be no legacy to learn from, and only a fortune to tempt or corrupt.

He had news for them all. They had left behind the makings for a little whirlwind of destruction, and as far as he could tell it couldn't have been any worse if they had just passed on the money in the first place. It would be interesting to see what Pam would do with the money once she got her hands on it.

"I'll get healthy as quickly as I can so you can be rid of me," he said.

"Why would I want to be rid of you?"

"I could say things like: you don't need me anymore,

or something as self-serving, but, I think the reason I need to move on is that you don't love me.''

"Really? You seem pretty sure about that.''

"I am pretty sure.''

She nodded. "But you love me.''

He gave that careful consideration before he answered. He had made love to her. He had been held spellbound by her beauty. He had traveled an undulating journey of emotional ups and downs because of her. But did he love her? "You know,'' he said, "I just don't know if I do or don't. Love has never been the focus of our relationship.''

"Exactly. I couldn't have said it better. So when you get out of here, let's make it the focus of the relationship and see what happens.''

"Just my luck, I take the job in California and we fall in love.''

"Why don't you take the job in Ashland and we fall in love?''

He imagined himself in this bed, looking like the sales rep for death, grizzled and wan, and probably smelling like a pharmacy. In contrast, she was a goddess. She was Kate Baker, only a new and improved model. If she could stand there, looking at him the way he must be and talk about love, well, who was he not to listen?

BETTY WEBB

DESERT WIVES

Arizona private investigator
Lena Jones is hired by a frantic
mother desperate to rescue her
thirteen-year-old daughter from a
polygamist sect. But when the
compound's sixty-eight-year-old
leader is found murdered, Lena's
client is charged with his murder.

To find the real killer, Lena goes
undercover and infiltrates the dark
reality of Purity—where misogynistic
men and frightened women share a
deadly code of silence.

"...this book could do
for polygamy what
Uncle Tom's Cabin
did for slavery."
—*Publishers Weekly*

*Available July 2004
at your favorite retail outlet.*

Detective Chief Inspector Neil Paget lies unconscious in a hospital bed after an attacker slashed his throat. But the investigation is stalled until a recovering Paget sifts through his tortured flashbacks while receiving taunting calls from a killer who has struck again. To solve a crime that is more personal than he ever imagined, Paget must venture deep into the dark pain of his own past...and the twisted mind of a killer looking for revenge.

"... pleasurable Paget police procedural....
Smith makes this case personal as the audience
gets deep inside the mind of the hero."
—Harriet Klausner

Available July 2004 at your favorite retail outlet.

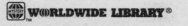

MEDUSA

SKYE KATHLEEN MOODY

A VENUS DIAMOND MYSTERY

U.S. Fish and Wildlife agent Venus Diamond
returns to Seattle when her twelve-year-
old stepbrother, Tim, is accused of drowning
nine-year-old Pearl Pederson while playing
aboard the family yacht.

Venus doubts Tim's story that a giant
jellyfish grabbed Pearl and dragged her
under. But when toxic venom is found in the
young victim's body, and witnesses spot a
giant sea creature roaming Elliott Bay,
Venus dives into its murky depths where her
probe leads her to the criminal elements at
the heart of the mystery—but not before
more deadly violence takes its toll.

"A fascinating crime thriller..."
—Harriet Klausner

"Venus Diamond is gutsy, hip, and truly
original—a rare gem."

—Janet Evanovich,
author of *To the Nines*

*Available August 2004
at your favorite retail outlet.*

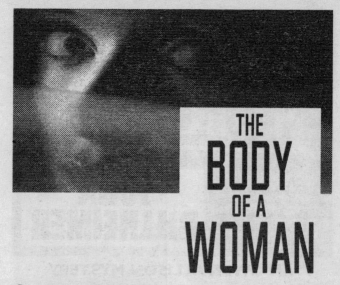
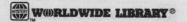

DRYBONE HOLLOW

JOHN BILLHEIMER

AN OWEN ALLISON MYSTERY

When a dam breaks in West Virginia, killing four
people and sending a black river of coal sludge
cascading throughout the region, failure analysis
engineer Owen Allison is asked to investigate.

But when a local woman goes missing, Owen
uncovers a dirty game of graft, corruption and
greed, which serve to mask an ugly truth that
someone will go to murderous lengths to hide.

"...a puzzle so ingenious that...readers shoulda
seen it coming—but they won't."
—*Kirkus Reviews*

"Billheimer spins a taut, trim tale..."
—Providence *Journal-Bulletin,* Rhode Island

Available August 2004 at your favorite retail outlet.

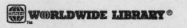

WORLDWIDE LIBRARY ®

WJB500